Written In Ink

Paul Newman

First published in 2023 by Blossom Spring Publishing
Written In Ink © 2023 Paul Newman
ISBN 978-1-7393514-5-8
E: admin@blossomspringpublishing.com
W: www.blossomspringpublishing.com

Chapter one

Canada

'If a man knows not to which port he sails, no wind is favourable.'

- Seneca -

October

'We cannot tear out a single page of our life, but we can throw the whole book in the fire.'

This quote from George Sand was the first thing I saw framed and hanging on the wall in a small wooden cabin I rented over the Thanksgiving holidays. I noticed this more than anything else because I was staying alone in this cabin to escape from everything and clear my head of the confusion about what was happening in my life. Or to undertake something more sinister.

I'm eighteen and just recently left high school. I'm confused about what to do with my life. I've tried asking my parents for advice, but they seem to have their own problems and are so busy arguing with each other they hardly even notice me. My so-called friends at school were so superficial that I couldn't ask them for advice. I don't seem to fit in at school or in society; I'm not the same as everyone else, and I can't find anyone on the same wavelength or mindset. As if that wasn't enough, I also broke up with my boyfriend a few days ago.

A friend of mine, my only good friend, really, says I'm introverted and that I overthink. She's probably right, and because I also think differently from most people, I tend to spend copious amounts of time alone – which I don't mind, being around too many people over-stimulates me.

I look around the cabin, trying to orientate myself to my surroundings, to where everything is situated. It's not difficult as there is only one room, and everything you need seems to be crammed into it. The table, chair and bed are made out of wood. I see where the stove is and some small logs next to it, which I'll have put into it and stoke up so I can boil some water to make myself a cup of coffee or tea. The stove is also a form of heating for the cabin. There's no running water, so I'll have to go down to the lake to fetch some. I notice a bookshelf against the far wall as I scan the room. I love reading, so the books look pretty inviting. I can't help myself; I must look at what's there. As I'm rummaging through them, one in particular catches my interest; it had fallen behind a mound of them stacked up on the top shelf. Mmm, the cover has images of various countries and stamps in different languages; it looks incredibly mysterious and intriguing. There are a couple of bookmarks inside. One of them, I can see, has a temple on it and 'Nepal' written along the side. The other one has some strange markings and 'India' written on the top. My curiosity is now aroused. I have to open it and see what it's about. I open it up – to my surprise, I realise it's a journal, handwritten with a fountain pen in an elegant writing style. The owner must have forgotten it; surely nobody would leave behind something as personal as this on purpose? Or had they not been able to find it as it had fallen behind this pile of other books?

I feel guilty that I'm looking at something quite personal to someone, and I know I shouldn't read any of it, but it's so compelling that I have to have a sneaky read of one or two paragraphs. I start reading extracts from various pages and realise that a woman started writing the journal while staying in this very cabin – also at Thanksgiving. I flip back the pages and start reading from her first entry in the journal. She wrote:

My husband and I have been drifting more and more apart over the last year. I was supposed to stay only four days over the Thanksgiving holidays here, but I came here four weeks ago. I decided to stay on longer as I felt I needed more time to be alone with myself. However, I'm not completely alone, as I have my dog, Scruffy, with me. After many hours of introspection in the last four weeks, I've concluded that I want to travel to hopefully find my authentic self. Before I embark on my big adventure, I've decided to write a journal of all the experiences.

Four weeks ago, I came here solely to get my thoughts together. I collected the keys from Mr. Smith at the hardware store, bought some provisions, and rowed out in a little boat to this small island in the lake. It only takes a few minutes to reach here from the mainland. It's not a big island, only one cabin and a small amount of wildlife. The birch and maple trees look gorgeous in fall, with all the leaves changing colour. There's no electricity or running water, but there's a stove I can put chopped wood into to cook and to boil water for coffee. There's an open fireplace where I make a fire to keep warm when it gets chilly. Quite cosy, really, basic but acceptable. I suppose you could say it's charmingly imperfect.

The first few days were strange being here alone, but after a while it was quite nice not to watch TV or go on the computer and to not have any distractions except my cell phone. At this time of the year it gets dark early, and there are no streetlights here so it's pitch black when it gets to about seven. But that's not a problem as I have lamps that take batteries. There's no noise of traffic; I only hear the crickets and owls at night here. The first day or so, I walked along the lakeshore and listened to the birds singing and the water splashing up along the shore as I contemplated numerous things. My daughter recently got engaged and didn't want to stay in Ontario, so she and her fiancé moved across to the other side of the country to British Columbia.

For the last eighteen months, my husband has been out of work, and he's finding it challenging to come to terms with not finding anything. He's becoming more and more irritable. Since then, my husband has started distancing himself from me. The romance had disappeared after thirty-nine years of marriage, and I felt melancholic most days at the mature age of fifty-nine. Seeing my daughter grown up, I felt a twinge of time *passing me by. I began to feel I wasn't needed anymore, as if I didn't have a purpose. I know they both love me, and I love them. However, I feel a void in my life, and I am desperately trying to fill it. I have spent so much of my life caring for others that I have neglected myself over the years. I feel taken for granted, I feel that nobody notices me or appreciates what I do for them. Perhaps I am overreacting because of the state I am in now; who knows?*

Last Thursday, I went down near the lakeshore with my easel, paints and brushes and painted a picture of the mainland. I also did some meditation on the veranda. Patients in the hospital used to tell me that by being creative – by painting, singing, making pottery, etc., – you are experiencing your soul, the real you.

I've tried breathing exercises, meditation, and yoga but none of that helped me from getting agitated with how I see the world going. I think *Nineteen Eighty-Four* by George Orwell and *Brave New World* by Aldous Huxley are playing out now in our society.

On Friday, I texted some friends to ask them for their advice on particular aspects of my life, but their advice didn't help. They meant good, but…

My husband and I never needed material things to make us happy; we were quite content and satisfied with the small things. We eat healthily and manage to do some daily exercise. We have a few close friends. Have a lovely house. We are proud of our daughter and love her very much. Her fiancé is a fine man; we couldn't ask for a better future son-in-law. However, I am becoming more dissatisfied with my work, and I feel it is making me dull. People have said that nursing is a noble profession, but I feel exhausted from all the years and effort I have put into it. Enough is enough; I've done my bit and need a rest now. I have the urge to get on and do something else, but what? I have started asking myself questions, like: are my friends genuine? Does my husband still love me? Does my daughter appreciate everything I do for her? Did I do enough for my parents before they passed on? I have started to doubt myself more and more nowadays.

One of my friends texted me and explained that as we get older and look in the mirror in the morning we notice mortality. We realise that time is slipping away. Our options and potential to accomplish things are deteriorating. I know it is not about being always happy – it is about being content and satisfied, feeling complete.

My husband and I are not materialists, we don't chase money or prestige; we have never had a big ego. We are satisfied living a simple life and are grateful for our health. I feel guilty and selfish for taking time out to be by myself. But my friend told me I shouldn't; it's just self-care. She was the one who told me to start journaling, painting, and meditating. She said I should re-invent myself, even have an affair... At my age? Re-invent myself and have an affair? Is she crazy? She thinks I'm a victim in the whole scenario. But I'm not. I just feel I should do something significant for myself before it's too late, and I'll regret not doing it. Perhaps I should have an affair?

During the day, I watch the geese flying south, squawking as they fly overhead. Some nights I sit on the veranda with a glass of wine and watch the sunset; it's so tranquil here, calm and relaxing. I've been rowing over to the mainland regularly to buy supplies. I've also gone into the town library to use one of their computers to research a few places I would like to visit. I searched on my phone, but the display was too tiny to see anything clearly. Some places are in England, as my husband is British and some of his family reside there. I'm thinking *of visiting them. Over the last weeks, I've tried to prioritise what I want out of life now. Certain so-called friends I want to cut away from. I've always feared people not liking me, so I've always said and done things to please them, to get their approval. But I don't want to live like that anymore. I want to quit my job; I've been doing it for many years, but what can I do at the age of fifty-nine? I'm sure nobody will take me on without any other qualifications or skills besides nursing. Will my attributes be enough? Who knows? I'm not even sure what I want to do. I'm too afraid to make the break and start something new, even though I would like to. Just, lately, I feel I've lost my way in life; I feel so empty.*

I have considered booking a cabin for my husband and me further up north for December, perhaps over the Christmas holiday. A change of scenery may do both of us some good. We could do cross–country skiing in the day, and in the evening catch up on reading one or two of our favourite books we have neglected over the last months.

A few nights ago, as I lay in my bed, I could hear the rain falling on the corrugated roof; I love hearing this sound. The sound of the rain hitting the roof put me into a semi-hypnotic state. I remember my husband telling me about when he served with the British Army (Royal Engineers). He travelled to Norway with his regimental ski team to train in cross-country skiing before participating in some competitions in Austria. When they came out of the cabins in the morning to start their ski training on the ski tracks, he told me everything was covered with freshly fallen snow from the night before. Everywhere was white as far as you could see. When they looked at the clear blue sky, there was not a cloud to be seen. And the contrast between the blue sky and the snow covering all the trees and log cabins made everything look clean. He said it looked phenomenal and was so still, so quiet, you could hear yourself breathe. That experience, he said, he would never forget. He used to tell me many stories about his travels; he enjoyed travelling. He was a keen runner, too. He loves adventure; he told me it was exciting to go into the unknown when he travelled, not knowing what to expect. It was like being a child again, experiencing stuff for the first time, and having a sense of wonder. I enjoyed listening to his stories of what he had done.

One windy morning here at the cabin last week, as I

drank my cup of coffee and looked out of the window, I watched the coloured fall leaves fall to the ground. It felt cosy inside the cabin, sheltered from the elements. I noticed the lake was quite choppy, too, so I thought I'd stay in and not try and row to the mainland to collect any groceries. Instead, I started to scribble some notes on a bit of paper. Where am I on the map of life? And where do I want to go? I need an aim, a goal in life of what I can do. At the moment, I just wish I had some romance and excitement back in my life. From reminiscing about what my husband told me about his travels, I decided I wanted to travel to England. Mainly because it is my husband's homeland. I got another piece of paper and wrote a 'bucket list' of all the places I'd like to see and the things I'd like to do. I decided I wanted, no, I needed to see and do the things I chose alone! I want to know if I can look after myself and not fear perhaps even travelling around Europe by myself. Just being self-reliant on me.

I had the money to do it from my parents' inheritance from when they passed on. The next step is to submit my letter of resignation to my workplace. The number of countries I wrote down on my 'bucket list' increased. I thought, this was outrageous; I couldn't do all this, plus *everything else I wanted to do, especially at my age. But if I don't do it now, then when? The countries I want to visit stretch halfway around the world. I calculated the time and money I needed to complete the trip. I'm pretty anxious about the whole idea and what my husband and daughter would think or say about the entire thing. I sat back in my chair and sighed. Scruffy looked at me with a confused look on his face. When I saw his expression, I smiled because he looked just as confused as I felt. At that moment, I received another text from my friend – she wrote:*

"'Memento Mori' is a Latin phrase that means 'remember that you will die'. It is intended to remind you of your own mortality, and the brevity and fragility of human life. Memento Mori can prompt you to take action and to avoid needlessly wasting the precious time that you have. It can help you put your problems in perspective. It can also help you cherish every moment in life and feel gratitude towards what you have.

"'Tempus fugit' is a Latin phrase that means 'time flies'. It is intended to remind you that your time is limited and continuously passing, both in general and when it comes to specific things such as pursuing your

goals or being with people you care about."

She's constantly texting me bits of information and quotes from various authors because I've always been interested in philosophy.

I stop reading and lower the journal into my lap; *what profound statements*. I ponder what this unknown woman is going through, which resonates with me. I wonder if my mother is going through something similar to this woman I'm reading about. Maybe I should also write a 'bucket list' to figure out what I want. Even though my parents are quick to dictate to me that I should get a job, and then get married, have kids and become a housewife, I don't want to be pressured into that.

Times are different now. My generation thinks differently from my parents' generation. I need time to figure out who I genuinely am and what I actually want. For as long as I can remember, my parents were constantly distracted by their work and their personal challenges with one another. I felt I was frequently intruding when asking for help or advice from them. I always felt physically and emotionally neglected. I thought I wasn't worth my parents' attention. This was probably the primary reason I spent so much time alone; I thought I was a burden. I also felt lost and abandoned, as though I didn't fit in anywhere. I was desperate to find out where I belonged and to have some meaning in my life.

It's getting dark, and there is a cold chill in the air; I have to put some wood in the fireplace and get a fire going to keep warm. I also have to put some wood into the stove to boil water for a cup of herbal tea. I'm doing all these tasks hurriedly as I am mesmerised by this woman's journal writings. I can't wait to start reading again. Eventually, I stoke the fire, put a blanket around my shoulders, and sit down with my herbal tea. I'm ready to start reading again…

That text from my friend was the push I needed; I had to decide. Choose to stay where I am, or go on a journey – an adventure of a lifetime! I just knew if I didn't do it, I would regret it for the rest of my life.

I see my life as seasons – from birth to twenty was spring, from twenty to forty summer, forty to sixty fall, and sixty to eighty was winter. I'm coming out of fall and into winter. If I stay healthy, perhaps I have another twenty years left. As a nurse, I have experienced many people on their deathbeds regretting what they wished they could have done but didn't. I'm not going to be one of those statistics.

I decided I needed three hundred and sixty-five days. That's how much time I calculated to achieve everything on my 'bucket list' – one year.

I had to sort out the visas I would initially need, then flights, accommodation, etc. The only thing I wasn't looking forward to was explaining what I was up to to my husband and daughter.

Well, it's Sunday today, and it's nine a.m. I know it's nine a.m. as I can hear the church bells chiming faintly from the mainland. I'm starting to feel anxious about the whole ordeal, as tomorrow my husband will take me to the airport. Since staying at the cabin, I've contacted my husband and daughter through texts and phone calls, letting them know how I have been feeling. The last conversation with my husband was lengthy and emotional, letting him know my plans for what I would do over the next three hundred and sixty-five days. He wasn't too impressed, but he reluctantly agreed.

Last night I sat on the veranda and looked at the clear night sky. I could see the masses of stars. They seemed so magical in the vast blackness of space; it was captivating. As I stared at the stars, I felt so small and insignificant. I had this epiphany that tomorrow I would embark on this vast journey across the Atlantic Ocean alone, without family or friends to accompany me.

While staring at the stars, I remembered my daughter as a small child waiting for me to come through the front door from work at night. She would run up to me with a big smile and hug me. She was always so happy to see me. It was an incredible feeling! Last night, I shed a few tears; I couldn't hold them back.

My husband sent me a text this morning with a contact list of some of his ex-work colleagues he used to work with when he was a Security Consultant after leaving the army. They live and work in some of the countries I will be visiting. He also contacted them to ask if I could stay with them for a short time or assist me with anything I needed. Doing this will help me save money to put toward my expenses.

I can't carry on reading; tears have welled up in my eyes after reading about this mother-daughter experience. It triggered something deep inside me; I felt a profound connection now with this woman. It was a powerful, emotional experience I had never felt before. I never had a loving, intimate relationship with my mother, and our connection was always awkward. I used to observe the stars on a clear night and was in awe. I can't seem to be in awe of anything anymore. I often wondered why people didn't think about things as much as I did – or maybe I hadn't met those people yet. Why am I so hypersensitive?

I get feelings about people and situations, an awareness that I can sense things about people and situations that others can't. I'm not sure if it's an asset or a liability. Sometimes it can become overwhelming. I see adults go to work for forty years, buy a car, and a house, get married and have kids. Then, at retirement, try and enjoy themselves for a few years before they succumb to some illness, which they will probably die of in the end. There must be more to life than that, surely. My best friend always says to me, "Don't think so seriously." I try not to, but I can't help it. Do I see the reality of life for what it is, and others don't? Is it me? Am I thinking too morbid? Or do I just not get it? My friend says, "Don't overthink everything; just be. Just accept it how it is."

I haven't always been like this. I remember many

happy times when I was a young child – so what happened? When was the transition from being that happy kid to how I am now? I can't remember – it must have been gradual, I guess. I yearn for that feeling again from when I was a kid. I used to think about time, how slowly it passed when you had to wait for something like Christmas. But, when I was happy, it was fleeting. How fast it passed when you were late for school! Time is unbearable when you are sad, and never-ending when you are in pain. All perception of time was determined by my feelings.

Chapter Two

England

'We have two lives, and the second begins when we realise we only have one.'

- Confucius -

November

Well, this is my first day in London. I got picked up at Heathrow Airport by an old army friend of my husband's, George. He offered that I could stay at his place while I was here in London. So I will for one or two days, but I promised my husband's cousin and uncle I would also spend some time at their place.

After George had met me at the terminal for arrivals, we went to one of the airport cafés to have a quick chat and get to know each other before he had to go to work. I could see he had a good sense of humour from that conversation. When we got to his car, I sat in the driver's seat instead of the passenger seat. Of course, I was surprised to see a steering wheel in front of me. George asked me sarcastically, with a smirk on his face, if I wanted to drive. I immediately realised the Brits drive on the left, and I got into the car on the right-hand side out of habit, as a passenger would just arriving from Canada. We both laughed. George's house is about a fifteen minute drive from the airport, not far away. He gave me a quick tour of the house when we arrived at his place, so I knew where everything was. He gave me his number to ring him if I needed help whenever I was in the city.

The train station is near George's house, so I get the train into the middle of London each day. The journey into London from here is approximately forty minutes; however, when I move on to my husband's cousin and uncle's place, the train journey from their home is only about twenty minutes. George gave me a tourist guidebook of London to help me find my way around.

I navigate London in a black taxi or a red double-decker bus, which is novel. This week I've seen the sights. I've visited a few museums and seen Buckingham Palace and 10 Downing Street. I've also had something to eat in the notorious China Town. I've seen a couple of gentlemen walking to work with bowler hats and pinstriped suits, which I've been told doesn't happen that frequently anymore. I also see children in school uniforms make their way to school in the mornings. This is surreal, because children in Canada don't wear school uniforms.

I bought a few items of clothing while shopping in the well-known Carnaby Street, which was famous back in the 70s for fashion. I spent some time at a coffee house in the lovely Covent Garden, where many nostalgic small shops and market stalls sell various things. Sitting there, I watched the people walk by doing their usual day-to-day things. I scanned through the London guidebook George gave me and found some interesting facts. In London, coffee shops were also popular three hundred years ago. Coffee was imported to England from Turkey in the Seventeenth Century. Crowds of businessmen had sat in these coffee shops and drank up to twenty cups of coffee a day. Johnny Gestang had delivered a weekly list of stock prices at 'Jonathan's Coffee House'. Fortunes were made and lost selling shares at the coffee shop; in 1773, the coffee shop was renamed 'The London Stock Exchange'. Now worth three trillion dollars. In London today, there are roughly one thousand five hundred coffee shops. And more people drink coffee now than tea.

But tea was also imported from China in the Seventeenth Century to England. Approximately six hundred small green wooden huts are scattered around London where taxi drivers can get a cup of tea and a sandwich. These huts can only seat about six people, though. London town also has about seven thousand pubs. One of the most popular drinks in England has been 'Gin and Tonic'.

There are many Indian restaurants in London, according to the guidebook, about two thousand. Since I have been in London, I have been out once to an Indian restaurant for a meal, but London can be pretty expensive. However, the aroma and the assorted spices tasted delightful. I am looking forward to being able to taste other various dishes when I arrive in India.

Today I will meet with my husband's cousin Robbie, who told me to meet him in Savile Row, where they create the legendary hand-tailored suits. On my way there, I will purchase the local newspaper to keep updated on what is happening here.

I was excited as I hadn't met any of my husband's family or relatives; I had only communicated with them through Facebook and WhatsApp. Apparently, there was a considerable amount of controversy between some of the family members years ago. Some events were shrouded in secrecy, leading to my husband breaking away from them. I will stay with Robbie, his wife, and daughter at their place for a few days. Robbie will take me to the rest of the family in north London over the next two days, Saturday and Sunday.

I had a great time with everyone – their hospitality was superb. Plenty of eating and drinking went on – with lots of laughter. They all have a good sense of humour. I explained why I was travelling, and they were all very supportive. By meeting up with my husband's family, we were all of the opinion that we could have a positive relationship with one another in the future.

Even though England is similar to Canada in a few ways, it's still noticeable they have a long tradition of old customs and are still patriotic and unique in their own right.

Today I'm spending the whole day and evening in a lovely hotel to treat myself to the spa, get a massage, etc. It's great, I can relax. However, I noticed the maids, waiters, waitresses, and doorman were invisible to the guests staying at the hotel. The people staying in the hotel were not rude; they just accepted them carrying out their *duties, and that was that. But while sitting in the lobby, it seemed we were all playing a role in a theatre. We are all actors and actresses playing a part. This was a revelation to me; this is how I felt back in Canada during the last couple of years while at work. Just acting, going through the motions, not really being me.*

Travelling has excavated childlike emotions in me – when a child is curious and experiences new things, they're rewarded with the amazement of what they have just witnessed. There are always surprises in our lives; how boring it would be if we knew the future. Travelling is constantly bringing up new experiences. As I sit in the lobby of my hotel, I quietly read my book of various quotes that I brought with me from the cabin. I will mark the ones I particularly like and perhaps insert them into my journal now and again, which correlates to the day or week I am having.

Tomorrow I will be travelling to East Anglia. Ipswich and Felixstowe will be the towns I will make my way to. My husband comes from Ipswich; he spent some of his childhood in New Barnet, London, where my mother-in-law spent most of her childhood. Felixstowe was where my father-in-law used to live until he passed on.

I caught the train at Liverpool Street station in London and arrived at Ipswich in the afternoon. I didn't have much luggage, just one small suitcase and a backpack; I thought I should travel as lightly as possible whilst I travelled between so many destinations in the short time I had calculated. Any essential items I need I can purchase at whatever location I happen to be in.

I got picked up by my sister-in-law from Ipswich train station. She took me back to her small cottage just outside Frinton. She lives there with her partner and six cats. Her partner was born in Birmingham. She is a teacher at the local school in Frinton. The cottage's location is lovely, situated in the typical English countryside. It was just how I imagined it: narrow country lanes passing through tiny villages, with the traditional red phone and post boxes and the local pub. My sister-in-law is a bit eccentric but has a good heart. She is always cracking jokes about something or someone. She promised to take me on country walks to show me the area. It seems strange listening to the radio in the car with English accents and watching English TV in the evening.

When I went with my sister-in-law to the pub on

Saturday night, we talked about the bygone days; some were happy times, and some were sad and unpleasant ones. We confided in each other about past encounters we had not told anyone else, and our conversations were somewhat cathartic. She explained a little of what went on earlier in her and her brother's childhood. I will write more about this later – I'm not feeling in the mood right now. I also mentioned to her about her brother being somewhat secretive about his work in some of the countries he had been in. He told me it was problems that he had to deal with and not bother me with. But his sister told me he never mentioned anything to her. But these secretive things that had bothered me over the years led to some of the friction between us.

My brother-in-law picked me up from Ipswich today to take me to his house in Felixstowe to spend a day or so with him and his wife. He owns a fish and chip shop in Felixstowe – so it looks like fish and chips are on the menu today.

After settling in at my brother-in-law's and having my fish and chips with salt and vinegar on them, I went with his wife to stroll along the seafront. I had to wear my other jacket, the pastel green one, as it was very windy.

Along the seafront, we spotted a tiny tea shop. We went in and had a cup of tea and a piece of walnut cake. It was delicious! We discussed how Canada and England were both similar and paradoxically different. We had a good chat there. The ambience was very cosy. An open fireplace with a few logs was burning away; a welcomed sight when coming in from the cold. The setting was fitted out so elegantly in the early 19th Century decor.

I will be getting the train down to Cornwall in a couple of days – the southern coast of England. When I get down to Cornwall, I'll have to catch up on my sleep. Each night we stay up late talking into the early hours of the morning.

On the train down to Cornwall, I met various characters who made small talk. One was an eccentric elderly gentleman who was astonishingly intelligent. As I sat next to him, he introduced himself as William, and I told him my name was Jane, and I had just recently arrived in England from Canada. Apparently, he was a professor who used to teach psychology and sociology at Oxford University but is now retired.

Ahh, finally, I know her name! Hey, Jane, I'm Sarah. Obviously, you can't hear me, but I feel obliged to introduce myself. At last I can identify this unknown woman with a name. Jane fits her.

I had spotted an old lady whose demeanour reminded me of Miss Maple, the fictional amateur detective character from author Agatha Christie. The people I've met and spoken to on my travels have been fascinating characters who all seem to have quirks and peculiarities, which I find extremely interesting. However, one woman I had noticed a few seats down from me irritated me for some reason. I don't know exactly why, but she seemed overly nice to everybody, which triggered something in me. I think it was because she reminded me of my second-grade teacher, Mrs. Reid; she was also so nauseatingly sweet to everyone.

I remember when I had to see the school counsellor, Mr. Kamanski. He told me that Carl Jung says we have to find our shadow side. We notice ours through observing other people, especially people close to us, and their insecurities and character traits bother us. The shadow or dark sides of us are beliefs and values we have suppressed deep down in our subconscious.

While the professor and I conversed, he mentioned the hormone dopamine. Apparently, our brain releases an incredible feeling of dopamine when we meet a need. However, it can be hard to stimulate once your basic needs are met. This is why people develop quirky habits of all sorts. Focusing on the needs of others can trigger dopamine, which can quickly become a habit. It may seem better than a gambling or sugar habit, but it has its downside. You can actually hurt those you wish to help if you take responsibility for meeting their needs and their own sense of responsibility is undermined.

This resonated with me; I told him this is how I am. So he carried on by explaining to me about altruism. And this was me, exactly. I asked him to repeat what he'd just told me so I could write it down in my journal.

Altruism makes us happy; researchers have consistently found that people report a significant happiness boost after doing kind deeds for others. Giving to people or charities activates brain regions associated with pleasure, social connection, and trust. Across the animal kingdom, animals cooperating with each other are more productive and survive longer. Altruism promotes social connections: when we give to others, they feel closer to us, and we also feel closer to them.

I mentioned my husband getting slightly depressed

sometimes because he was out of work for so long. He recommended a book he believes would help him, Lost Connections *by Johann Hari, so I'll purchase a copy as soon as I can get to a bookstore. As we approached the station, where we both had to get off and go our separate ways, he said, "Mood follows action. It starts with behaviour, then thoughts, feelings, perceptions and sensations, in that order." And with that last bit of advice, he wished me a good day.*

I get a scrap of paper and find a pencil lying on the bookshelf and scribble down what the professor said. I find myself on this journey of self-discovery, now, just as much as Jane.

I'm staying in a tiny Bed and Breakfast in a quaint village on the coast. There's a grocery shop that doubles up as a post office, a few houses, and the proverbial pub. The locals are friendly; in England, people are always willing to exchange a few words with me, commenting on the weather or just giving a nod of the head and wishing me good morning or afternoon. The B-and-Bs tend to cook the guests a full English breakfast in the mornings; they taste delicious, but I'll have to stop eating them soon as I'm putting on weight. I'll also have to start cutting out the tea and cakes in the afternoon! Well, I don't have to give up the tea and cakes too quickly.

Many thatched cottages are in the villages along the coast in the south of England. There are many small coves with fishing boats, too. I'm so happy I decided to come to Cornwall; walking along the beach is good therapy. It's the end of November and getting colder by the day, but I feel content and satisfied. But I must admit I'm slightly anxious about travelling through Europe, but I'll worry about that later.

As I sat on a bench looking out towards the sea, an elderly couple sat next to me; we talked about this and that. Then a young woman about my daughter's age walking her dog sat beside us.

We ended up talking about how our respective generations perceive things. The elderly couple expressed themselves by saying they valued time, and that resonated with me. They said they felt many families no longer sat down for a meal together at lunchtime, or for dinner in the evenings. The sense of family and belonging had been lost. But the young lady interjected and said that's how life is now, with both parents having to go to work to pay all the bills. The elderly couple half-heartedly agreed *with her; they knew she was right that our society has evolved to where we find ourselves now. The elderly couple went on to say that they think integrity, honesty and loyalty have deteriorated over the years, and most men are no longer gentlemen, as they used to be. The young girl gave her interpretation of how she saw things. I just listened to them. But in the typical British style, the couple got up, grinned and said, "Well, now that we've put the world to right, it's time to go home and have a cup of tea." The young girl also got up and carried on walking her dog. It was just small talk between everyone, but we shouldn't underestimate people's time when they pay attention and speak to us. They are being vulnerable and giving a bit of themselves to you through what they say and do. And vice-versa; that's the start of how people bond. Also, paying attention to and participating in your partner's hobbies and interests, which they love and have a passion for, is selfless; it's considerate and thoughtful for your partner. Being vulnerable is the way to genuinely communicate. That relationship usually can flourish better than being cagey, not being trustworthy of people, and not being naively vulnerable.*

I stayed on the bench and enjoyed the view of the sea.

Then, I read a few more pages of my book and found a quote that I thought was fitting to write in my journal to sum up the day.

'You have your way. I have my way. As for the right way… it does not exist.' Fredrich Nietzsche.

Being influenced by reading the journal, I am urged to say something to my mother about my pent-up frustrations and emotions, which I need to express. I'll send a text to her to try and explain how I feel. I have emotions that I've repressed for a long time, and I need to allow them to surface to express myself:

"Mom, I'm texting you something. I hope it makes sense to you.

It appears to me as we grow up, we start losing ourselves in some way. We build walls around ourselves because we are afraid to show people our authentic selves in case they ridicule us or won't like us and have nothing to do with us, and we will be left alone. Changing ourselves to fit in only enhances that critical voice. The stress of becoming someone we are not is enormous. It starts eating away at us, and feelings start getting bottled up. Sometimes, I lost that sparkle, that unique spark, and it disappeared completely as I grew up. I had a confusing and rebellious relationship with you and Dad growing up.

That's the thing about receding into our shells; we don't realise we're pushing our parents and friends away. But you haven't really been there for me, physically or emotionally. You haven't... I feel as if I'm alone in a small rowing boat out on the vast ocean with no land in sight. I feel abandoned and confused... So now I'm trying to get back to you and Dad."

Ahh – just my luck – there's no reception. I'll have to try and send it again later.

If I ended my life, would anyone care or miss me? I sometimes feel like I don't have a purpose or reason to be here. I don't have a talent; I'm not good at anything specific. I don't stand out in the crowd – I'm just ordinary. I get the impression that nobody likes me. Would I amount to anything later in life? All you hear about on TV is how badly the economy is doing, and, with over seven billion people in the world, the narration of not having enough resources to ensure our survival. Humanity appears to be constantly living in fear over something or other. I haven't seen any hope for me or my generation for the future. Everything seems to be a struggle. I've lost interest in everything I used to enjoy. I don't see the sense of doing anything anymore. So why does reading Jane's words make me feel a little better? Even enough to stop me from ending my life? I think it was Jane being, at her age, still willing to try and search for something. Something I gave up doing long ago. Also, her relationship with her daughter. A connection I so desperately wanted and needed too with my mother, but one that never materialised.

I'll have to go outside to collect more chopped wood for the fire and stove to keep warm and make some coffee. I have to admit I'm captivated by Jane's story, and I feel something has awakened within me.

I am so intrigued by Jane taking on such a challenge at her age. I can't imagine my mother doing anything like this, and Jane's adventure has only just begun. I wonder how Jane will cope with travelling through Europe. I better get back in and get the stove stoked to make some coffee and start reading again.

Chapter Three

Europe

'Twenty years from now you will be more disappointed by the things you didn't do than by the ones you did do. So throw off the bowlines, sail away from the safe harbour. Catch the trade winds in your sails. Explore. Dream. Discover.'

- Mark Twain -

December

I've arrived at Dover; it's late afternoon, and I've checked into a small hotel on the seafront. It's nothing special, but I just need a room to sleep in, as my ferry departs tomorrow at ten a.m. I've taken a stroll along the pebbled beach, and I can see the famous white cliffs of Dover. They look remarkable. The simplicity of just strolling along the beach is perfect for my mind; there's nothing to distract me, and I can let the past weeks sink in. I am relishing this time by the sea, connecting with nature again, smelling the salty air as my time in England ends. When I am in Europe, I will be in big cities again.

This was the first town my husband got based at when he started his army career. There are a few small pubs and fish and chip shops along the harbour. I bought a bag of chips and was walking along the beach when a seagull swooped down and stole a chip right out of my hand. I was so shocked; I didn't expect that. Some people walking towards me looked on in amusement and told me it always happens along the seafront.

I walked into town to find the café where my husband said he used to go with some of the other guys from his squadron. But apparently, according to some locals, it had been torn down, and there's nothing there anymore. This seaside town looks a bit shabby and run down to me, unlike how my husband described it. Perhaps he was more interested in the young women back then than the town itself.

I made my way to the port, where I would get the ferry tomorrow. I managed to see the last of the foot passengers and the last three or four cars drive onto one of the ferries, which would sail early this evening. Walking back to my hotel it was dark, and I could see the lights on in the pubs. I peeked in the window of one of them, and I could see some of the fishermen dressed in their rugged clothes having a well-earned drink and one or two elderly men smoking a pipe. You could smell the aroma from outside through one of the open windows. I like to smell the aroma of a pipe; it reminds me of when I was a child and went into a small room where my grandfather was smoking his pipe while writing his books.

I'm feeling trepidation regarding tomorrow, but I'm simultaneously excited to see some new countries. All the European countries I will visit will speak different languages. However, I've been assured that they all can speak English as a second language.

When I returned to my room and started getting ready for bed, I noticed a small frame hanging directly over the bed's headboard. It depicted a man and woman in medieval times in a stance, both holding a longbow ready to shoot an arrow. And directly underneath them, there was something written:

'Your children are not your children. They are the sons and daughters of life's longing for itself. They come through you but not from you, and though they are with you, yet they belong not to you.

You may give them your love but not your thoughts, for they have their own thoughts. You may house their bodies but not their souls, for their souls dwell in the house of tomorrow, which you cannot visit, not even in your dreams.

You may strive to be like them, but seek not to make them like you.

For life goes not backward nor tarries with yesterday.

You are the bows from which your children as living arrows are sent forth.

The archer sees the mark upon the path of the infinite, and He bends you with His might that His arrows may go swift and far.

Let your bending in the archer's hand be for gladness; For even as He loves the arrow that flies, so He loves also the bow that is stable.' Kahlil Gibran.

Reading that, I trembled with emotion; I had to sit on the edge of the bed for a while. The truth and wisdom in which it was written pierced my heart. I know it made sense, but I love my daughter so much it's not easy for me to let go. But if you genuinely love your child and you have unconditional love for them, that's what should be done. You have to give them the freedom to experience life in their unique way. Mistakes and flaws included.

Well, today is the day. I boarded the ferry and found a comfortable seat next to the window. As I look out the window, I can see the white cliffs of Dover fading away into the distance as the ferry sets its course for Calais, France. For the crossing, I will read a chapter or two from one of the books I've brought along. They have a cafeteria, a shop, and a small bar on the boat. All the vehicles are parked on the decks below. I've acquired a discounted train ticket online, which allows me to travel through Europe.

I talked with my husband on the phone just before I boarded the ferry, and he told me some good news. A couple of weeks before I left Canada to head to England, he tried again to arrange with his buddy to go into business together by having a small coffee shop. They had talked about doing this for some time now. Having his own coffee shop has been a prominent dream of his for quite a while, but now it appears they've decided to finally go for it. I hope it works out; there's no real reason it shouldn't. Hopefully, this will give him purpose and meaning back in his life. Not finding work for so long got him down, and he felt dejected. However, he's always been personable and well-spoken, so I'm confident the coffee shop will succeed. Not to mention his business skills and, of course, quality coffee. He always told me he would work in his coffee shop with 'Meraki', which I thought was his buddy. After some time, I discovered 'Meraki' was a Greek word for doing something with total love and pure soul. It is leaving a little piece of yourself in your creative work. I burst out laughing when I found that out!

During my first few days in France, I noticed many people were reluctant to speak English with me. For any assistance, I have to ask the younger generation. They are willing to speak English. I visited the Eifel Tower in Paris. I spent some time at an elegant café watching the people walk past, thinking how romantic it would be in the summertime with couples sitting outside at the cafés lining the streets of Paris. However, I didn't feel as comfortable travelling through France as in the UK. The French are inclined not to talk as much to strangers as the Brits are. But who knows, perhaps it's the time of year when the trees are bare, and the weather some days can be unforgiving. It's enough to make anybody feel a little discouraged.

I will travel through Belgium, Holland, and Spain over the next few weeks. However, I want to visit their renowned Christmas markets in Germany just before Christmas. So I'll spend Christmas and New Year in Germany, then move on to Portugal to travel along the entire coast in January.

I've worked out and prepared for some of the trip in Portugal, but I'm going to be spontaneous in what I do and test my creative thinking. So that should be interesting? I have some uneasiness about that.

December is not the best time to travel through Europe; everything seems dreary and dark. It would have been better in the summertime, but it wouldn't have fit in with my plans. So I will be travelling through Europe and staying at Bed and Breakfasts'.

As I travel through Europe on the train, I find it challenging to communicate with people, unlike in the UK where their mindset was that a stranger is a possible friend. So instead I look out of the train carriage window at the landscape to soak up the European scenery. I read a little from one of my books and write a few more sentences in my journal.

As I stare out the train window, I reminisce about past events and people from my childhood. I think of my parents and how caring they were; I had a happy childhood. Not like my husband; he had a rough one. I think of how I am now; I'm no longer an attractive young woman. I'm an ageing, semi-attractive woman with wrinkles who is slightly overweight and will be sixty next year. I'm starting to doubt myself – is this trip even worth doing? I'm feeling homesick, and I miss my husband and daughter. I'm also feeling tired from travelling already. The thought of all the places I still want to visit and the time it will take is starting to overwhelm me. So I will read more from my book to take my mind off things. It's funny how you miss the little things from home. I miss listening to country and western music and eating a hotdog in a bun with lots of relish and mustard.

When passing through Belgium, I stopped off and bought some of the famous Belgium chocolate, which is constantly being discussed back in Canada on how lovely it tastes. I had some gift-wrapped for my daughter, and I couldn't resist trying some myself. It tastes delicious! I found the main post office in the town centre of Brussels and mailed my daughter the chocolate with other souvenirs I had picked up in England.

One of Agatha Christie's famous fictional characters was the great Belgium detective Poirot. However, to my amusement, they spoke about him as though he was a real person when mentioning his name.

I don't spend too much time in Belgium and head to Holland. While in Amsterdam, I was amazed to see so many people riding bicycles. I go into a 'coffee shop' to sample some of their cookies while having a well-deserved cup of coffee. Since I've been travelling, I don't drink half as much coffee as in Canada, and, when I think about it, I probably drank too much then. On the wall was a picture of Van Gogh, and underneath was a small plaque which said: 'A famous Dutch painter who painted 860 oil paintings in his time. Born in 1853 – died in 1890.'

After eating some of those delicious 'cookies', I felt utterly relaxed and without a care in the world. No wonder, after I found out what the ingredients were. I'm amazed at the sizes of the greenhouses in Holland full of flowers. I'm sure in the summertime it must look incredible to see all the fields of tulips. The windmills scattered around the countryside gave it the character I envisaged Holland to be. Most Dutch people can speak fluent English, and are uncomplicated and easy to get along with.

I am in Germany now visiting Hameln, the well-known 'Piped Piper town'. I'm staying with an old army buddy of my husband's. His wife will take me to the town centre to look around and do Christmas shopping.

We ate bratwurst (German sausage) and drank glühwine (mulled wine) at the Christmas market. It's spectacular to see all the various Christmas stalls selling typical German food and winter ornaments. The atmosphere is phenomenal. There is a light covering of snow everywhere; it has a natural Christmas feeling. Carollers were singing Christmas carols outside the town hall. Tomorrow I will go to what was known in the Cold War as East Germany and visit the legendary Checkpoint Charlie. I will return and spend Christmas with my husband's old army friend and wife. He decided to stay in Germany with his German wife when he left the military. Germans apparently open their presents on Christmas Eve. I will miss my family at Christmas, not being with them. Like so many other people who are working over Christmas have to do. For example, military people, *police, doctors and nurses, etc.*

I tried enjoying Christmas day, but I missed my family more than I expected. New Year was good watching all the fireworks and the people out on the streets singing and enjoying themselves. But, shortly after midnight, I went to bed. It's not the same if you're not with someone you love, friends, or family members.

I understand why my husband enjoyed himself in Germany while he was based here. The people are friendly and look forward to any event they can use as an excuse to eat, drink, and be merry.

I fly to Portugal the day after tomorrow. I've genuinely enjoyed my time here in Germany.

I have been looking forward to not being with my parents for Christmas and the New Year for once. I used to imagine what it would be like to take off someplace where nobody knew me and to celebrate Christmas and the New Year there, someplace where everyone was happy and genuinely enjoying themselves.

January

The day I was flying to Portugal from Hanover airport, I lost my passport. Back in Canada, I'm forever forgetting where I put my car or house keys and leaving things to the last minute, – which causes stress – and I have to rush to get to work on time. While in the airport ladies' room, I put my passport down next to the sink to wash my hands and then left it there. A woman came rushing after me with my passport in her hand, saying something in German to the effect of, "You've forgotten your passport, you silly so-and-so." If my head wasn't screwed on, I'd probably forget that as well. Luckily, my passport wasn't lost forever.

I landed in Lisbon and surprisingly got through customs rather quickly, unlike at Heathrow, London. Now that I'm in Portugal, I will travel from Lisbon to Porto by train first, then by bus, then bicycle, and then on the last leg of the journey by hiking. After that, if I have time, I would like to travel up to Santiago in Spain by train or bus.

My husband wrote to me, empowering me with encouragement, saying I have many attributes: courage, perseverance, adaptability and resilience. And I shouldn't forget this, as they will get me through any difficult times I might endure. He also wrote: "Always remember, you are braver than you believe, stronger than

you seem, and smarter than you think. I'm proud of you."
Reading this gave me a massive boost of confidence and
motivation, which I needed at this stage of my journey.

I stayed a few days in Lisbon. Whilst there, I noticed
some English books on display in an old shabby
bookshop window, so I went in and browsed through
some of them, and I found a couple that interested me. In
one of the books, a paragraph caught my eye:

'What's it like to be a woman? We are sisters, mothers
and wives. We know secrets and the truth within the
family. We give birth to life, mother nature in her glory.
We take on most of the worry so others may have
unburdened lives. We are the homemakers, and we try to
keep the family together. We are yin, and men are yang.
We are soft, yielding, receptive, passive, and reflective,
whereas yang is hard, active, assertive, and dominating.'

Nowadays, many people wouldn't feel quite that way,
and the LGBTQ community, I am sure, wouldn't agree.
Things have developed into a more complex society these
days, and that's probably why I'm struggling to conform.
When I read the comments on social media about me
from the students who were in my class, I wonder if I'm

really as intense as they say. Or are they the ones who are so insecure in themselves that they have to act and talk the way they do about me?

I travel along the coast by train, looking out to the sea; I love the ambience of travelling by train, it has a certain nostalgia about the entire experience. While seated, you can feel relaxed and stare out the window while having a coffee and a sandwich, read a book or newspaper, or converse with people. There is no effort involved like driving a car, were you have to concentrate, pay attention to traffic, etc. On a train, you can sit back and enjoy the experience. I've managed to phone my husband and daughter on Sundays at a time we agreed on, so they knew I was alright and had no significant problems. I always feel in a tug of war with myself, between returning to the role of mother and wife while simultaneously trying to reconnect with me. How will I find myself when I am constantly confronted with the past?

Since I departed Canada, I've had many feelings that surfaced more intensely than I imagined. Everything sounds great in theory, that you would like to undertake aspirations in your life, but it's not as simple as you think when it comes to actually doing it. Fear holds a lot of people back – also the courage and the leap of faith that is needed. The sense of responsibility and loyalty can deter some people from carrying out their ambitions, dreams or desires.

As I look out of the window, I see the wind blowing the tufts of high grass on the beach and kids playing outside; it's getting dark, and they are probably not realising the time because they are so immersed in enjoying themselves. The carefree moments of childhood, eh? This reminds me of my childhood. We played outside until dusk, and our parents had to call us in before it got too late. For most kids, their childhood is a carefree time to enjoy themselves without having all the responsibilities you do as an adult. That wasn't the case for my husband; I often wished he could have had a more enjoyable childhood. Whilst I've been writing, the train began to slow down and has now come to a complete stop. I slide open the window and look out to see what the problem is. I can hear the wind blowing; I search for a word on my phone to describe the tufts of long, dried grass swaying in the wind on the beach. Ah, I've found one. 'Susurrus' – a low soft sound, whispering or rustling of a quiet breeze.

I remember a sense of freedom and contentment playing with my friends as a kid. Perhaps contentment is the only real wealth. Maybe as adults we should not forget two words in the morning before we go about our business: 'Carpe Diem' – seize the day.

I reach the town of Nazare. I will spend a few nights here, and then I will carry on with the second leg of my journey in Portugal by bus.

I'm presently staying in a guest house with a perfect view out onto the sea.

I walked around the tiny cobbled roads and looked at the small shops. It was very calm and tranquil, with just a few people wandering around. On the beach, I noticed some fishermen fixing their fishing nets besides their boats. I sat next to an old wooden shack, read one of my books, and jotted down a few lines in my journal about what I observed around me. And that brings me to now. I feel content and satisfied as I take deep breaths of the salty sea air. The atmosphere is soothing to my mind. It's as though time has slowed right down in this village, and the bustling world of the work environment in big cities around the world is still carrying on. I feel a twinge of guilt that I am not working or contributing, but at the same time, I think I have done my part; it is time for me to rest now at this stage of my life. My mind tends to wander as I sit here, and various thoughts come to mind. I'm concerned, perhaps even afraid, of what I might discover about myself on this journey. Maybe I have a dark side to me, which can be dangerous. I hope not. But who knows what we are capable of if the circumstances present themselves?

As I sat there, I reflected on my journey so far. Until now, I'm satisfied with how things have gone. But although it's been enjoyable until now, I still have this underlying feeling that something will happen that I'm not ready for. When I embarked on this journey, I knew I would immerse myself in the unknown, but I was still compelled to do it anyway. A sort of paradox; I wanted to do it, but I didn't at the same time. They say you should listen to your heart more than your mind. Well, that's what I've done. Intuitively, I believed it was the correct decision. Only time will tell, eh?

People say we don't have to worry; we have all the time in the world to do what we want. But that's not precisely true. Time is infinite, but our life is finite. If we stay healthy enough to live a reasonable life, we must fit *everything we want to experience into approximately eighty years. So people put off what they can do today and say, "I'll do that next year," or, "When I'm a pensioner, I'll have time to do that." But the thing is, life gets in the way; illness crops up, or financial problems, and things you want to do get put on the back-burner. Then, eventually, you end up not doing or saying the things you wanted to. I know this because I've often experienced this with patients lying on their deathbeds. They confess they wish they hadn't spent so much time working, that they should have spent more time with their children or grandchildren, travelling, or doing something they were passionate about. But they didn't; now they regret it. We shouldn't allow ourselves to end up in that position where we regret many things we didn't do or say because of whatever excuse we told ourselves. When I return to Canada, I will have a conversation with my daughter and make sure she realises this. I feel all parents are obligated to their children to pass on any knowledge they have to try and help them. It's up to the children if they take it on board or not, it's their choice, but at least you know you tried to help them the best you could.*

My parents always dictated what I could and couldn't do. They didn't give me any constructive advice to help me. They didn't empower me to do anything; I always had to search for information. To me, their mindset is old-fashioned.

It got pretty chilly sitting there, so I returned to my room and packed my things for the next leg of my journey with the bus. Being out the whole day in the sea air yesterday made sure I slept so well last night I almost didn't hear my alarm this morning. Sitting on the bus, I stare out the window and watch the waves roll in. I'm in a sort of daydreaming state, just enjoying the bus ride, not having to think about anything in particular except when I jot down a few sentences in my journal of what I'm experiencing. Finally, I reached my destination, stayed overnight, and prepared for the next leg of the journey – the fourth leg of hiking. My small suitcase will be taken to the hotel where I will be staying, and it will be stored in a room ready to collect when I get to the hotel in Porto.

I finished the last leg trekking on the trails next to the coastline while observing and hearing the waves rolling in hypnotically; it was so refreshing. The sea is a great solace. It's so vast and timeless; it puts everything into perspective. When I'm with nature, my soul sings. Even though it was a crisp January day, there was a lovely blue sky with just a few clouds. As I was hiking, I met very few people on the way, probably due to the time of year. The hiking part of the journey along the coast was solitary, a private matter between me and the sometimes lonely path I was plodding along. Many thoughts were going through my mind. The primary one was: what if I return to Canada and haven't figured out who I really am and what I want to do with the rest of my life? I started to panic, thinking of the worst case scenarios. I must stop overthinking, otherwise I will drive myself crazy. I must take it one day at a time.

The hiking was arduous, and I had an enormous sense of pride and fulfilment at the end that I accomplished it. I checked into my hotel, had a shower, and put some clean clothes on. I'm now relaxing outside on the terrace with a small glass of port wine, which is actually produced here in Porto. I've arranged with the hotel to hire one of their Vesper scooters so I can ride around Porto to see the sights.

As I rode around on my Vesper outside of Porto

through the narrow winding roads, I almost drove over a guy near a lighthouse. I was going too fast, and he was walking back to his place in the middle of the road. I swerved to miss him and almost ended up in a ditch. He came rushing over to see if I was okay and apologised for nearly causing a fatal accident. He suggested that I sit down on a stool he had near his front door before I decided to carry on driving. Apparently, the lighthouse was his, and he'd had it refurbished into the living quarters in which he lives. After apologising to him profusely about me almost running him over, he told me he had a Bistro which he owns in Porto, and that I should come there sometime and have a drink on the house. I said I would take him up on his offer.

I met him at the Bistro and had a fascinating evening. His name is Francisco, he is fifty, charming, tanned, good-looking, and comes originally from Mederia. His character was charismatic and captivating, and I have to admit I was attracted to him. During the evening, he was trying to impress me, coming out with comments such as, "Amor-Fati," and, "Be yourself; you never know who will love the person you hide."

His English was quite good, with a slight accent that

was endearing. Throughout the evening, he tried to impress me with some English words he had learnt over the years. 'Forelsket' – the euphoria you experience when first falling in love. 'Trouvaille' – something lovely discovered by chance. 'Discombobulated' – emotionally confused or uncertain. When he used this word, it made me smile, and I wanted to laugh. But I managed to hold it back. Then he told me he'd come across a specific Japanese word: 'Ukiyo' – living in the moment, detached from the bothers of life. It seems as though he's a person who likes to articulate himself with words, which I felt somewhat appealing. With the way he dressed casually, and with his three-day beard and cavalier manner, he was totally intoxicating.

It's been eight days since the near accident with Francisco. We've been meeting up at the Bistro regularly to have meals, drink wine, and talk about anything and everything. At the moment, it's a platonic relationship, and that's fine; after all, I am ten years older than him and married. But I'm concerned it could turn into something more, as he sometimes indicates with certain glances.

One evening he invited me to the lighthouse for a meal

and a glass of wine, but it ended up with more than one glass. He suggested that I sleep there and not return to my accommodation, which I did on the condition he sleeps in a different room. And, as the perfect gentleman, he did indeed sleep in a separate room.

The following day after breakfast, we went walking along the beach. Over the last couple of weeks, I've felt alive again, excited. I noticed I was enjoying this way of life – perhaps a little too much. I hadn't felt like this for a long time. While walking along the beach, he mentioned that earning or having up to a certain amount of money is okay, but it doesn't play a significant role in your life to be happy. All we need is the fundamental stuff; the rest is a bonus. He was a minimalist; he didn't believe in owning so much clutter. He liked living a simple life. To be spontaneous and live in the moment. Don't overthink and worry so much about the past and the future. Which is fine if you're single and have no kids, like him. He can come and go as he pleases and do what he wants in his house. But if you're married, have kids, and have a home, could you still live that lifestyle? What does it mean to feel whole and fulfilled as an individual while sharing a life with somebody else? These are the sort of questions I *have been asking myself.*

One particular thing he said as we walked along the beach impacted me. He told me to stop and say this specific phrase and take a minute or two to think about it. "I am what I think you think I am." Then he went on to say that people don't see or think about you as you assume they do. So, I put it to the test and asked the staff at the hotel and some of the guests, who I've gotten to know over the last few weeks, how they perceived me. Every single person perceived me differently.

I could relate to this from the school I used to attend. My peers in my class perceived me differently regarding how I thought I was. Many students didn't see me as 'normal', or as society portrays normal. If you act or think differently from other people, they seem to be afraid of that; and the hierarchy definitely doesn't want you thinking autonomously, as they class that as a threat to them and what they represent. I'm not sure who I could ask that I trust to give me an honest answer about how they genuinely perceive me, but I would be curious about what they say and why. I get many people judging me on social media, and they don't even really know me, not truly. Some tried bullying me online, but I ignored them;

I couldn't be bothered wasting my time interacting with them to defend myself. I suppose it was the easy way out.

It's the third week of being in Portugal, and as I carry on seeing this guy Francisco, I notice the relationship is developing into something serious. I have mixed emotions; I know I should break this off before it gets out of hand, but, at the same time, I want it to carry on. I'm feeling guilty that I want this to continue. But now he has asked me to stay here in Portugal for a few more weeks and not carry on travelling. My emotions are all over the place; I'm confused and can't think straight. I sense if I stay on, I'll live to regret it, I'm sure. I feel a different 'Me' emerging, and I'm trying to suppress it because I feel guilty regarding my husband.

I want to call someone to get advice on all this emotional confusion. I can't contact any of my friends or family about this. But I still have the business card from the professor. I could phone him; we got along fine on the train. I'm sure he could help and give me some advice. Knowing him, the advice will be more than likely intellectually rationalised, but it's better than nothing.

What is she doing? The stakes are too high for her to gamble on staying with this Francisco guy! If she decides to get more involved with him and her daughter finds out, she'll jeopardize their close relationship, never mind her relationship with her husband.

After trying to get through to him by phone a few times, he finally answered. I felt so ashamed while talking to him about my story, but I felt so mixed up that I had to speak to someone about it. Finally, after hearing my story, he agreed to help me.

He explained that hormones and their influence distort my views on things. For example, love triggers dopamine, serotonin and oxytocin. That's why it's so motivating. Dopamine is the great feeling you get when you find your missing keys, and it's the neurochemical that's evolved for seeking and finding. Animals sniff around for food and mating opportunities, and dopamine surges when they find something that meets their needs. But the surge is short. Dopamine does its job by dropping after it rises, so it's ready to alert you to the next chance to meet your needs.

You don't expect that great dopamine to last when you find your keys. But when you find 'the one' you make so much dopamine that you assume you will soar forever. Then, when the dopamine finally subsides, you'll wonder what's wrong. You might even blame 'the one' for having changed.

Oxytocin is a powerful hormone that we can feel surging through our bodies when we hug, kiss, and feel loved by someone. It's the neurochemical implicated in trust. The more oxytocin you release with a person, the more attached you feel. More touch, more oxytocin, more trust. But trust gets complicated in the human brain. You trust someone to live up to your expectations and don't realise how complex your expectations are. Eventually, your loved one fails to meet your expectations, and you fail to meet theirs.

To your mammal brain, any loss of trust is a life-threatening emergency. Oxytocin dips, and cortisol surges when a sheep is separated from its flock. Cortisol is the feeling we experience as fear, panic, or anxiety, and it works for sheep, motivating them to reconnect with the flock before they're eaten alive. In humans, cortisol turns disappointment expectations into emergencies.

Serotonin is getting respect from 'the guy'; it feels good because it stimulates serotonin. Social dominance brings more mating opportunities and more surviving offspring in the animal world. Animals don't dominate because of conscious long-term goals; they dominate because serotonin feels good.

Your brain always wants more respect to get more serotonin. Your loved one may give you that feeling at first by respecting you or helping you feel respected by others. But your brain takes the respect you already have for granted and wants more respect to get more good feelings. Some people constantly make more demands on their loved ones, and others continuously seek higher-status partners. We'd all be better off if we understood the origins of our neurochemical impulses.

I thanked him for his help, and I was right; I knew he would have a logical answer for my situation. However, maybe a bit too analytical and intellectual for my liking. Something was still missing, which probably only a woman could have told me. So, after my conversation with the professor, I phoned Francisco and told him I would be travelling up to Santiago, Spain, by train, and I would be back at the end of January, so I would see him in one week. I said this to win me more time to see how I felt about things.

After travelling along the scenic coast of Portugal and Spain, I eventually arrived at Santiago. The well-known painter Salvador Dali who used to paint bizarre images was from Spain. Initially, I wanted to visit some museums here, but I don't think I feel up to that anymore.

I have one week here to get my thoughts and emotions figured out. I haven't called my husband and daughter for the last two Sundays as I was so involved with Francisco and had my phone turned off the whole time. So I will call them tomorrow and let them know I am safe and now in Spain. I'm sure they are starting to think something has happened to me, like an accident, and that I am in a hospital. This is where responsibility and loyalty kick in as my default.

I couldn't really take in the sights and enjoy myself in Santiago, as I was overthinking. I telephoned Francisco, and as we spoke, he promised me how amazing it would be if we stayed together and lived on the coast. He made it sound so easy and carefree, the life we would be living. I could see my old life drifting further and further away, and I could imagine my new wonderful, exciting life with him. But I told him it's just a fantasy; we imagine a dream life we would like to have, but it can't become a reality. He wouldn't have it; he kept pleading with me to stay. I tried to explain to him this was just lust, not true love; we had only known each other for a short time. I had become tired of my old life, but I knew this would never last. My husband and I had too many memories over so many years for them to be thrown away so quickly. Surely this isn't the real me I was looking for. He was becoming impatient and angry with me, and I started crying. Part of me wanted this new life, but the other part knew this was wrong. I told him I would travel back down by train to see him.

I couldn't do this to my husband and daughter; it just wasn't right. It shows me that if the circumstances are a particular way, the dark side of us that we are afraid of starts to surface. I've decided to fly on the next leg of my journey to Dubai, and not travel back to Porto. I've written a short letter to Francisco explaining that I'm carrying on with my itinerary and then returning to Canada. Not many people write letters anymore, but I'm still old school. I mailed the letter from the airport. I have to prepare myself psychologically for the next stage of my journey. I have to put what happened in Porto to the back of my mind; otherwise, I won't concentrate, and I'll make mistakes like forgetting my passport or missing my flight. The last couple of days has been draining after all the emotions I've been through. So, Jane, compose yourself now.

I expect the Middle East to be this Lawrence of Arabia *experience. The anticipation of how it will be makes my heart flutter, unlike before entering Europe. This part of the world that awaits me seems more exciting, and I feel it has a particular mystery and a hint of adventure. This is taking me to the next level, pushing me out of my comfort zone, so much so that perhaps I can get at least a glimpse of my true self.*

Just a few minutes before I was due to start boarding the plane, I had a message from my husband telling me that my best friend was going around to our house to see him and ask him if he was alright while I was away. She mentioned that she could cook for him or help out somehow if he wanted. This was my best friend, who had been texting me while I was staying in the cabin, encouraging me to travel and not wait until it was too late in life, and suggesting that I should have an affair. She's divorced and constantly chasing after men; I wouldn't put it past her to try something with my husband. Knowing her, she'll suggest a 'quid pro quo' – something for something. He said he wanted to tell me about her when we were on the phone while I was in Spain but was concerned that I would get angry and that he didn't want to upset me. I can't reply to him now as I am on the plane, and the stewardess has asked me to turn my phone to flight mode. So, I'll have to wait until I arrive in Dubai to contact him.

I had this flash-back to when I was a teenager. Some girl at school made me angry about something or other, and my mother said to me, "Any person capable of angering you has a hold over you; they can anger you only when you permit yourself to be disturbed by them." She tried to give me motherly advice at the time, but I didn't take it in. It's strange how emotions and feelings can trigger a distant memory from your past. But, this time, I will take my mother's advice and not let this so-called friend of mine in Canada disturb me and trigger my emotions.

I thought Jane was going to risk her family and career on Francisco. I'm so relieved about her decision to not stay with Francisco; I think that would have only carried on being suitable for so long, and she would have regretted that decision for the rest of her life.

Chapter Four

Middle East

'The world is a book, and those who do not travel read only one page.'

- St. Augustine -

February

Arrived in Dubai today. I won't need a jacket here; it's 25°C. Very welcoming, after just coming from a chilly sub-zero Europe.

As I flew into Dubai airport, we passed over the man-made tree-shaped Palm Jumeirah Island, known for glitzy hotels, high-quality apartment towers, and upmarket global restaurants. Dubai is the largest city in the United Arab Emirates. It is located on the southeast coast of the Persian Gulf in the Arabian Desert and is the capital of the Emirate Dubai, one of seven emirates that make up the country.

Dubai is known for luxury shopping, ultramodern architecture, and lively nightlife. However, I think I will be giving the nightlife a miss. I haven't got the energy that I had when I was twenty. *Arabic is the official language, and while on the flight I learned some Arabic from my pocket handbook of Arabic phrases that I purchased at a travel agency in Porto. But I shouldn't have any problems as their second language is English. The currency is UAE dirhams (AED). Islam is the official religion, so I will be respectful of its rules and regulations. Dubai is unrecognisable from how it looked fifty years ago; it's completely transformed since then, by looking at the pictures in the handbook.*

Since I've been in Dubai, I've noticed I haven't seen any elderly people; the age group seems to plateau off at about fifty years of age. This makes sense as I've been informed by my husband that Dubai is a transient city where people come on a contract to work for a few years and then return back to their original country.

I visited the Mall of the Emirates; it has an enclosed area where you can actually ski, which is weird when you think that the temperatures in summer rise to 50°C outside. I took some photos of the Burj Khalifa – it cost one and a half billion dollars to build and is eight hundred and thirty metres in height. The colossal fountain attraction near the Burj Khalifa is also spectacular to see, especially at night with the lighting and music responding to it shooting high up into the air. I also saw the Luxury hotel Burj Al Arab, which cost one billion dollars to build and stands on an artificial island two hundred and eighty metres from Jumeirah Beach.

On Dubai creek, there are many dhows with produce being unloaded on the key. I spent some time going on a relaxing walk on the lovely white sand of Jumeirah beach. The temperature was perfect for a walk; in the summer, you wouldn't dream of walking or sunbathing on the beach as the temperature is too high. I've been told, besides wearing hats, that some Chinese and Filipino women who work here use umbrellas to keep the scorching sun off them. I think I'll start doing the same.

I've been strolling through Madinat Jumeirah; it's an Arabian five-star resort designed to resemble a traditional Arabian town – it was like being transported fifty years back in time to how it used to be. With the modern, vibrant Dubai surrounding this resort, it's quite noticeable how far this country has come in a relatively short time. The sensation I felt as I walked through the streets of this resort replicated my expectations of how it would be here in the Middle East. I'm sure there will still be towns like this in other parts of the UAE, like Qatar or Oman, which I can't wait to see. Then I visited the Souk at Deira; the gold souk was huge. Dubai Aquarium would be something to see, but there's not enough time to see and experience all the attractions here. It's so overwhelming here for me; it's a culture shock. Such a massive contrast from how and where I live in Canada. Parts of Dubai are so modern, with futuristic architectural designs. It is noticeable that Dubai has money because it has evolved so quickly over the last fifty years. Living here is on a whole different level. Not at all what I'm used to. It's as though I'm in a school playground, and I've walked away from the familiar part of the playground where I've always played and wandered into the unfamiliar territory where the big kids are. I feel out of place, like I don't belong here.

I missed my coach to Abu Dhabi, so I decided to take a taxi, which surprisingly wasn't that expensive. My taxi driver informed me that taxis are relatively cheap throughout the UAE, so that will be the mode of transport I will be using for my entire stay here.

I arrived at my hotel, the Crowne Plaza on Hamdan Street, right in the centre of Abu Dhabi. According to my *taxi driver, Dubai is mainly for the younger people, and AD is more for my generation; it's more relaxed and laid back than the lively, fast-paced Dubai. Dubai, over the years, has gotten more touristic and is orientated towards the younger generation. He also told me most of the taxi drivers in the UAE are Indian, African, and Pakistani, like himself. The workers here in the UAE are predominately Indian, Bangladeshi, Filipino, and Pakistani. The managers are mainly westerners. In the UAE, you can experience one extreme to another – the wealth gap is very apparent. From workers with minimal status and few belongings on a low salary to the Emirates of high status and much wealth. It's mind-boggling. After completing their military service, some British military guys came to work and live in the UAE, as my husband did. Hotels are the main focal point for westerners to meet up in on Thursday evenings to have a drink; alcohol is forbidden anywhere else. They usually arrange to meet and have brunch together on Fridays or Saturdays.*

Abu Dhabi is the capital of the UAE. Years ago, men used to earn a living from pearl diving here. Now AD produces eleven percent of the world's oil. I walked all along the Cornish until I got to the Marina Mall. Along the Cornish there were a few shops selling snacks, renting bicycles, and one or two cafés. I had a chicken shawarma to eat; it tasted very nice. It is similar to a wrap.

There is not much in AD compared to Dubai, except hotels with a bar. AD is a bit more traditional than Dubai; Dubai is more orientated toward the younger generation. I will make my way to Al Ain in a day or so, as I want to experience more of the indigenous people and their traditions.

With a taxi, I moved from the Crowne Plaza Hotel to the Regent Hotel on Saadiyat Island, about ten minutes from AD. It's a great location, directly on the Persian Gulf. I saw a brochure on Saadiyat Island that looked so alluring that I wanted to treat myself by staying here. The ambience in the evening seemed so sophisticated and elegant that I couldn't resist booking a room. It's expensive, but I'll cut back on other things later to balance it out.

I travelled by bus to Al Ain, which was cheaper than a taxi.

Al-Ain is a fertile oasis located approximately one hundred and sixty kilometres east of Abu Dhabi. Its name, The Spring, derives from its originally plentiful supply of fresh water, making its way underground across most of the plain lying before the Omani mountains. It's also known as The Garden City. The hotel I'm staying at in Al Ain is the Rotana. I must say, all the Arabian food tastes exquisite. Compared to Dubai, I have noticed that more women in AD and Al Ain wear the hijab and abaya, and the men wear dishdasha. I reflect on that. I respect local customs, but I ask myself how I would feel if I had to dress and live this way all the time.

As I am travelling by taxi around Al Ain, I can see there are small shops where men are smoking Shisha and drinking Moroccan tea inside, but also outside underneath the shade of some trees. The weekend starts on Friday, and Friday morning they all make their way to the nearest mosque to pray. You can hear the call to prayer five times a day. Most people do not work and tend to relax on this day.

I've purchased some expensive Frankincense perfume for myself and my daughter. In most hotel lobbies here, it's an Arabic custom that dates and Arabic coffee are served to welcome the guests.

In February, here in the UAE, it's creeping up to

30°C. Apparently, the temperature will stay like this for a few months, then start climbing steadily in July, where it will reach 50°C and remain so high for a few months.

In the hotel Rotana where I am staying, I met a group of students from the UK who have just finished their studies and are on a gap year travelling before they pursue their designated professions. One young woman told me that some have studied anthropology, psychology, and sociology, and some want to be teachers. There are approximately seven or eight of them altogether. While chatting with two or three of them in the lobby, one woman asked me if I was interested in joining them on a two-day 'Arabian Experience', which was booked to take them out into the desert tomorrow. First, I declined – they were all young adults, and I was old enough to be their mother and was afraid they could not relate to me. However, they insisted, so I eventually agreed. After all, being surrounded by bright young people should also help me rejuvenate my mind.

We got taken out by the hotel's 'Tourism Expedition Travel Department' to a campsite just outside Al Ain by a convoy of land cruisers. There were about six jeeps with all the equipment and belongings. The short expedition was named 'The Arabian Experience'. This could be the Lawrence of Arabia *experience that I was wishing and hoping for all along. Camels were delivered by open-top trucks to the location in the desert where our base camp would be, which we would be riding on over the next day or so. At the campsite, the marquees, where we will be sleeping, were erected by a team of guys. A campfire was prepared and a meal was made consisting of goat and biryani rice, accompanied by Arabic coffee and Moroccan tea. We were all sitting or lying on intricately woven carpets two metres long by one metre wide. There were Emiratis with some of their children sitting with us around the campfire, telling us stories about their heritage and customs; it was very informative. It was a strong feeling of belonging, like a family. It was incredibly satisfying. This is how the nomads used to live. There was a sense of being united, and you could speak freely with one another and help each other deal with challenges in your life.*

We talked and expressed our opinions and thoughts on various subjects as the evening progressed. With all these intellectuals, some of the conversations got very deep and sophisticated, as you can imagine. We were inclined to talk with the people nearest us during the evening. The guy and woman beside me asked why I had travelled alone from Canada. Since they were complete strangers, I somehow didn't mind explaining the events leading me to rent a cabin in Canada and spend four weeks there for introspection. I disclosed how I felt there and what I was trying to achieve on this trip.

After hearing my dilemma, they felt obliged to try and help me somehow. From what they had been studying at Uni for the last couple of years, I couldn't ask for anybody better, to be honest, from an intellectual standpoint. I mean, what did I have to lose? Nothing. I told them I feared being forgotten about, ignored, or replaced. The woman next to me told me this is called Athazagoraphobia. She said, in her opinion, she thinks it's good that I've made the decision to travel. She went on to explain, and I quote, "One of my professors at Uni told us that the radius of how far you travel diminishes as you get older. First, you travel to other countries, then your own country, then your region, neighbourhood, and eventually the shops near your house, then only your home. Like friends, as time passes, you notice who your real ones are, and you tend to stay only with them. One *by one, they move away or pass on, your children have children of their own, and with their work, they tend to spend less and less time with you until eventually you are left with just your partner, then when they pass on, you are alone." There was a short silence, and I reflected on what she had told me. Then she continued.*

She referred to something from Thich Nhat Hanh: 'We rarely offer ourselves the time and space to consider: Am I doing what I most want to do with my life? Do I even know what that is? The noise in our heads and all around us drown out the still, small voice inside. We are so busy doing 'something' that we rarely take a moment to look deeply and check in with our deepest desires.'

I liked this quote. This is why I brought my book of quotes along with me on my travels; the few sentences I read from each section seem to put things into perspective for me to understand. I asked the woman and guy next to me if I could read something from my journal which summed up how I felt after months of travelling. They agreed and listened inquisitively. I read:

"We are afraid to be ourselves, including me. We don't think we are good enough. When we look in the mirror, we believe we are not pretty enough, thin enough,

smart enough, etc. If only we didn't think like that, we would lead a different life. I often ask myself: if I had no fear what story would I tell others about myself? But first, I would have to confront that fear. What am I so embarrassed and ashamed about? I am slowly waking up to how I would like things to be in my life. However, awakening is a painful process. Foods don't taste the same. Conversations are different. The pain is caused by shedding my former self for my new one. To lessen the pain, I must surrender. I have to be okay with not being okay. Let the unfolding happen. For not only am I awakening to a new world, but I'm also awakening to my true self."

They both smiled and nodded their heads. Then the guy on the other side of me said, "I've recently read something on the internet, if you're interested in hearing it."

I said, "Sure, why not?"

He told me he came across this article while he was researching something for his studies. He searched on his phone until he found it again. As he read it aloud, I wrote it down in my journal:

'We should let go of the people unwilling to spend time with us. Stop having challenging conversations with certain individuals who don't want to change. Stop being with so-called friends who have no interest in our presence; they steal our time, energy, and mental and physical health. If we are excluded, insulted, forgotten, or ignored by the people we give our time to, cut away from them. We are wasting our energy and our life. We are not for everyone, and everyone is not for us. The more time we spend trying to make ourselves loved by someone who doesn't want anything to do with us, the more time we waste, depriving ourselves of having a connection with someone who wants to interact with us. Some people should just not be in our lives. The most valuable things we have are time and energy; both are limited. When we realise this, we begin to understand why we are so anxious when we spend time with people in activities and places that don't suit us. We should make our life a safe haven where only 'compatible' people associate with us. We must decide that we deserve true friendship just by being who we are.'

He also mentioned something about Teleology and Axiology. Teleology is the study of purpose and meaning;

it is the study of telos, which is the highest value. Axiology is the philosophical study of goodness or the worth of something.

That information had a profound impact on me. It made complete sense. It was so surreal, being in the desert in the middle of nowhere halfway around the world, thousands of kilometres from home, sitting around a campfire listening to a complete stranger explain something so honest and raw. After travelling and searching for an answer to the questions and doubts I had in Canada, this seemed to put everything into perspective for me. What are the odds of me travelling all this way and meeting someone to read this to me? Some people would call this synchronicity or serendipity.

There was silence, and you could sense that we were trying to digest what he had just read. Even though these students are highly intellectual, one thing I had more than them was life experience. I asked them if I could pass on some wisdom that I had written down in my journal. It was about what I've learnt and heard from the various people I've met over the years, especially in the last few months. They both agreed and listened in anticipation:

"We may think we completely control ourselves. However, a friend can easily reveal something about us that we have absolutely no idea about. Environment influences you, starting when you are a kid. Life is a book, and the chapters are the different stages in your life; I'm entering the last few chapters of my book. Time is a fleeting concept, and you have to make sure you use it wisely. Every day you have to pay attention, or else it will slip by you without you noticing. Prayer is when you talk to God, and meditation is when God talks to you. What movement does for the body, stillness does for the mind. You can turn things around. You can completely recreate yourself; nothing is permanent, you're not stuck, and you have choices. You can think of new thoughts, learn something new, and create new habits. All that matters is that you decide today and never look back. Being different isn't bad; it means you're brave enough to be yourself."

They didn't say anything but smiled and nodded in appreciation.

The woman was curious about my husband and daughter. She asked me if I could tell her something about them, and I said, "Sure," and began to describe them to her, starting with my husband. For me, he is the ideal man.

"He has brown hair, slightly greying, and blue eyes," I said to them. "He's a loner who doesn't need people to have a good time. But with the people he likes, he can be friendly and pleasant. He's flexible, he can adapt to most circumstances and adjust to the personalities and environments he desires to be in. He is himself, regardless of who is watching or interacting with him. He is a good listener, as he understands the value of silence and respect when others speak as a mutual courtesy. He gives importance to content rather than volume. He is self-aware and knows his good qualities, and also his flaws. He can see right and wrong in complex scenarios. He is a critical thinker who analyses all aspects of the issue before passing judgment. With rusty social skills, he does not disguise his intent with flowery language or flattery. He can fit into a friend group but not rely on them, he is quite happy and content being on his own. He decides his future and knows he is responsible for himself, his actions, and the consequences. He has a small but close social circle on the same wavelength and can also be trusted. He is self-sufficient and will do his best to be utterly self-sufficient in all aspects of life. He does not want to rely on anyone for the basics in life. He is not afraid to take risks. He is not an attention seeker."

I showed them a photo of my husband and daughter, which I kept on my phone.

She – the student – replied, "Wow, you have a lovely family; it sounds like your husband is an interesting man. I sincerely hope that with your experiences and the people you meet on your travels that you can resolve any questions or possible regrets you have about your life. The trade-off of taking time out to travel and reassessing your life is worth it. They call it an 'opportunity cost'; you obviously can't be back in Canada with your family and friends by being away for a certain amount of time. However, I believe the cost is worth it."

I wanted to talk about my daughter, but I knew I wouldn't be able to stop if I started. Not only that, but everybody was making their way over to the marquees where we were going to sleep; one was for women and the other for men. So, we decided to call it a night and get some sleep, ready for the next day's activities. The woman was still curious about my daughter; she asked me if I would describe what she is like to her the next day, *which I agreed I would.*

The next day I found out that the woman I spoke to had studied psychology, and she was extending her studies to become a behaviour analyst, and the guy had studied philosophy. The students reminded me of hippies in the late 60s and early 70s, with their ideas and philosophies toward life; they were like an updated version to me.

The Emiratis put on a show with falcons, and then we rode on camels a small distance to where we got picked up by the jeeps to go wadi bashing – basically, driving up and down the sand dunes as fast as possible without tipping over. It was exhilarating. When we stopped, we sat underneath some palm trees for shade, and had coffee and dates. Sitting underneath the trees with the desert surrounding us, you couldn't hear any noise; it was utterly silent. This solitude and the warm air blowing lightly over our faces felt spiritual, as if you could sense or hear ancient advice and guidance from the elements. The world I hear when it's quiet has a simplicity about it; the stillness feels real.

After that, we drove up to Fujairah in the middle of this mountainous terrain and then circled around to make our way back to Al Ain. The next day, I will hire a driver and a vehicle from the hotel to drive me to Muscat, Oman, which is three hundred and fifty kilometres from Al Ain.

A massive sandstorm is heading our way, so we had to delay our departure to Oman, as most of the road we would have been travelling on was in the open. Even though they have shrubbery lining the road to combat light winds blowing sand onto the road, this sandstorm will cover the road in no time. Apparently they will send vehicles out after the storm to clear the road, like our snow ploughs clearing snow in Canada. So, I will stay at my hotel until I get the green light that it's okay to travel to Oman. I noticed one vehicle pull into the hotel car park, and the whole left-hand side of the vehicle was stripped of paint. The person had travelled from Oman to Al Ain, and the sandstorm, blowing from the east to the west, had taken all the paint entirely off one side of his vehicle.

Today, I received a message from my husband that a friend he worked with in the UAE years ago arrived in Abu Dhabi last week to conduct maintenance work on the UAE Land Forces' indoor weapon systems in Abu Dhabi and Al Ain. My husband has arranged that he meet me at my hotel to have a coffee and a chat. Before he arrives, though, I have to search my room again, as I have lost my house keys and my purse; there's not much money in the wallet as I keep most of it locked up in the room wall safe, but it's still annoying as I always misplace things or lose them.

In Al Ain, compared to Dubai and Abu Dhabi, western women must keep themselves almost completely covered as to not offend the local's beliefs and religion; everyone complies. So, I have to do this and not forget, but I get tired and sometimes can't concentrate with all the travelling, and that's when I start forgetting and losing things. I have enjoyed travelling, but perhaps underestimated what I can do nowadays; I am not thirty anymore.

Charles, the former working colleague of my husband, who now resides in Montreal, Canada, met me in the lobby of my hotel. While having coffee there, he talked about when he and my husband were working together in the UAE.

He mentioned that when they first arrived here, they had to hand in their passports and deal with a lot of *paperwork criteria to get their residency ID cards. That was the time my husband's father died of lung cancer. It was a race against time for the authorities to process the paperwork and hand his passport back so he could travel to England for the funeral. But everything in the Middle East takes time; you must learn to be patient here. At the same time, there were some anomalies with their work contract, which had to be sorted out. While this was happening, they lived temporarily in a hotel and searched for permanent accommodation. The possibility of not being able to go back for his father's funeral bothered him considerably. He was getting anxiety attacks and couldn't concentrate properly on the tasks at hand. Time ran out, and it wasn't possible to make it to the funeral as he couldn't get his passport back from the authorities in time. That was devastating for him; he felt he didn't have closure. Charles said they eventually found an apartment and started work, but he said sometimes when my husband went into Abu Dhabi, he had blackouts for an hour or so and had no recollection of what he had done during this time. He used to forget where he'd parked his car. One time he couldn't remember where he lived and had lost his phone, so he checked into a hotel to not have to sleep outside. After that, he always carried a piece of paper with his address, so if it happened again, he could show a taxi driver who could bring him home. It did happen again, and after that incident, he visited a doctor in Abu Dhabi to find out what was going on with himself. The doctor explained that his father's death and so many other things he had to deal with at the time was information overload; his brain shut down like a computer crashing. But there were contributing factors adding to his symptoms, which Charles didn't know about. It was suppressed memories and emotions from his traumatic childhood. Only months later, when both of them went to Oman for a weekend to have a break from work, did my husband tell him that some experiences from his childhood had resurfaced that he had suppressed for years.*

I was shocked, utterly taken aback by what Charles had told me; my husband had never told me any of what had happened in AD. I was speechless; I didn't know what to say.

Charles suggested we go through to the bar and have a drink. You can only get alcohol in hotels in the UAE, and it's costly, but I needed a drink after hearing all that.

Charles offered to drive me to Muscat, Oman, as soon as the roads were cleared.

I have just received from Ali, the portier, that the roads are being cleared now. It is still quite early, and since I packed my belongings last night, I will get some breakfast with Charles before leaving for Muscat. I will try and get back to the journal tonight.

The next day the roads were clear, and Charles drove me to Muscat. He took me to the same place where he and my husband stayed. It was a thatched hut with a bed and a small wardrobe at an exclusive holiday resort. Approximately ten of these huts were close together, about one hundred metres from the beach. He reassured me that as much as people believe that the Middle East is dangerous, Oman and the UAE are two of the safest places in the world. We had lunch at a seafood restaurant along the promenade. Afterwards, Charles drove back to Abu Dhabi to catch a flight back to Montreal, Canada, the next day.

Later that evening, I walked along the beach towards the souk; the warm sea breeze was so soothing on my face that it made me feel like I didn't have a care in the world. I love the marketplaces; I find them stimulating.

It's very laidback here. The people are easy-going and friendly; I didn't think it would be such a relaxing atmosphere. I'm pleasantly surprised. There's not much to do in Muscat; everybody is just going about their typical day-to-day lives. I spend a few days relaxing on the beach to recuperate from travelling and save some energy for the next phase of my journey – Qatar. Until now, I have not had much time to be alone or contemplate as much as I intended.

I'm sitting outside a well-weathered, tiny establishment on the promenade which sells tea and Shisha. I'm enjoying a small glass of red tea, and there are two Omani gentlemen further down smoking flavoured Shisha. The aroma wafts down to where I sit, and it smells delightful. I wear my headscarf and light material garment to cover myself, which I purchased in Al Ain. The two gentlemen look on, smile slightly, and nod to acknowledge that I was respecting their traditions and religion. I can hear the waves rhythmically crashing onto the shore as I stare out at sea, and this sound I find incredibly therapeutic.

As I sit here, I reflect on my experiences, feelings, and emotions from the start of my trip until now. Has travelling helped me know what I want from the last stage of my life besides seeing the countries I always wanted to visit? At this stage of my journey, I would say yes and no. I'm a third of the way in, and I've had more questions than answers so far. However, from all the characters I've met and talked to in the various countries, they have definitely given me food for thought. It makes me wonder about the people who leave their own country, friends, and family to immigrate to a foreign country to live there permanently. I'm sure to have a better quality of life, but it still must be an emotional and difficult thing to do. But, also, courageous.

When I left Canada a few months ago, I naively thought I would have an epiphany about my life. Well, that didn't happen, did it? Hopefully, over the next eight months, that will change. Sometimes I still doubt whether I've made the right decision to spend so much money on this voyage of discovery, advancing into the unknown to find something that will satisfy my anxiousness and uneasiness with myself. We all have to take responsibility for our lives; we can't blame others. I feel a hint of shame that I'm spending this money on myself and not sharing it with my husband and daughter. But I know if I don't pay attention to myself now, I'll regret it for the rest of my life.

I've rested enough physically, but I have to mentally prepare for the next stage of my travels, which will be to Qatar. There's only one flight a day to Doha, Qatar; it's a short flight, approximately one and a half hours.

I arrive at Hamad International Qatar airport and get a taxi to take me to my accommodation, 'Ezdan' – block one. Apparently, there are five blocks in total. It's situated in the West Bay area. There is a tour bus I will be taking to visit the prevalent sights of Doha tomorrow. Doha is Qatar's capital and most populous city, with a population of about two million. The city is located on the Persian Gulf coast in the east.

The tour bus, which was only half full, departed West Bay and headed to The Pearl-Qatar. The Pearl-Qatar in Doha is an artificial island spanning nearly four-square kilometres, built on a former pearl diving site. It is now a modern district with a wide range of sports, entertainment, and shopping opportunities. The Katara Cultural Village was also on the route, great for shopping and eating. On the way back, we drove alongside the corniche, the beautiful boardwalk that stretches seven kilometres along Doha Bay. From there we could observe the Imam Muhammad ibn Abd al-Wahhab Mosque. It's a spectacular building to admire. We stopped at the Museum of Islamic Art, too. Then we carried on to the lively, centuries old Souq Waqif near the corniche, which was once a trading centre for the Bedouins, who used it as a camel market, among other things. You can now find many interesting goods from gold jewellery, to colourful fabrics, and bronze lamps, like those in One Thousand and One Nights.

We then visited the Falcon Souq. Falconry is an old Bedouin hunting technique. A monthly auction sells the most sought-after birds for tens of thousands of dollars. At the souq, you could smell the aroma of frankincense. People use its oil on the skin and in aromatherapy. Frankincense oil seems to kill some types of bacteria and fungi; it is commonly used as a fragrance in soaps, lotions, and perfumes. We could see the boats called dhows in the bay as we came out of the souq.

It's unbelievable the pace at which Qatar is being built up. From the early 70s of pearl diving and small fishing villages, it has evolved, primarily due to its gas and oil reserves, into a metropolis. I have to say I've *enjoyed and relished the time I've spent in the Middle East, and my expectations have been fulfilled. But to keep to my schedule, I will soon have to prepare for the next segment of my journey: India. I will stay in a compound in New Delhi, where the British diplomats reside. My husband arranged this with an old friend who works in the visas and passport section at the British embassy.*

I'm looking forward to the flight as I want to relax and read one of my books.

One thing that had helped me for many years was reading books. Some of them were for escapism, but others drew me into the story as if I was the main character and helped me deal with the reality of my life – just like Jane's journal. Travelling to all the various countries and interacting with the indigenous people stimulated something in Jane that was always in her but needed prodding to make her aware. By noticing this, it's as though I have been jolted out of a deep slumber, and, for the first time, I am seeing things differently in my life. If I hadn't found Jane's journal and started reading it, I would have more than likely followed through with ending my life. I had a suicide letter already written and in an envelope with 'Mom and Dad' written on the front.

What had actually stopped me from carrying through with my sinister plan? It was that passage when Jane described coming through the door in the evenings and her daughter running up to her and hugging her with delight. That made me doubt myself. That was the pivotal point where I was hooked and decided to continue reading to the end.

Jane, to me, has integrity; she can act according to relevant moral values and social and cultural norms. I admire her open-mindedness and willingness to consider and accept new ideas, opinions, or perspectives. She's definitely an inspiration for me to get my act together. She's earned my respect by doing what she's doing at her age. Of course, she has weaknesses and makes mistakes, but don't we all?

Chapter Five

India

'All the flowers of all the tomorrows are in the seeds of
today.'

- Indian Proverb -

March

To use the four hour flight time from Doha, Qatar, to
New Delhi, India, well I read the pages I printed out from
my research on India, which I had done in the hotel's
business centre in Qatar.

I arrived at New Delhi airport, where my husband's
friend John picked me up to take me to the British
compound where I would be staying – it's near the
British embassy, too. It was quite an experience on the
way to the compound. The hustle and bustle of so many
people, the traffic, and the vehicles swerving in and out
and honking their horns seemed like complete chaos. But
to them, it was organised chaos.

India has a population of 1.32 billion people. New
Delhi is the capital, and it has eleven million. The life

expectancy in India is about sixty-eight years. The main religion is Hinduism, and the language is Hindi. I will use the Indian Rupee (INR) over the next few weeks. The largest employer in India is the Indian railways, and Bollywood is also a well-recognised industry.

After sorting myself out in the spare bedroom at John's place, Vicky, his wife, showed me where everything was in the compound. There is an outdoor swimming pool, a sort of country club with a bar where they can serve you the typical gin and tonic, and, at three p.m., they even serve tea and cakes. It is noticeable there has been, and still is, a British influence on this country. Workers are tending to the flowers in the immaculate gardens. They have a small shop where you can purchase some typical British food items. You can't drink the tap water here, though. Most people who work at the British embassy live in this compound. As I peeked out through the bars of the big cast-iron gates at the entrance to the compound, I saw the Indian children in school uniforms walking past on the street alongside cows. Cows are considered sacred in India. As I continued to peer through the gates, I watched bicycle rickshaws pass, and, across the street, I could see street vendors selling curries; the smell of the food made me feel hungry. I will spend the rest of the day recuperating from my flight, as tomorrow Vicky said she will show me around New Delhi.

So, this morning Vicky and I took a tuk-tuk around the busy, hectic city. I knew there was poverty here, but it has an astounding effect on you when you experience it first-hand and up close. It makes you realise how lucky we have it back in Canada. We went to a restaurant where she knew the owner, and we had a delicious curry. After lunch, Vicky took me to a local market where I bought a few traditional clothing items, which I will wear while I'm staying in New Delhi. Apparently, tonight we will be going to a massive outdoor party with some of John and Vicky's friends. According to Vicky, there will be many VIPs going.

We have just returned from this massive party – it was a few kilometres outside New Delhi in a vast field. As we approached the venue, I could see this very long line of cars in front of us, which at first I thought was traffic, but it wasn't; all the vehicles in front of us were turning left into the parking area of the venue. They were obviously the guests. There were hundreds of cars. After we had *parked up, we made our way to the entrance, and we had to show our unique entry cards. There was orange ambient lighting everywhere simulating flames, lighting the casino tables and areas with extensive buffets where you could help yourself to whatever you wanted. There were bars with all the alcoholic beverages you could imagine strategically placed all around, and live bands playing music. John and Vicky introduced me to people they knew. Bank managers, airline pilots, Embassy diplomats from various nations, entrepreneurs who got very rich through their endeavours, businessmen, Bollywood actors and actresses – anybody who was anything was there. There must have been three to four hundred people. The atmosphere was electrifying. Such a contrast in lifestyle, compared to what I had seen earlier in the city. At midnight they had a huge firework display. I've never experienced a venue anything like this before in my life! It was outrageous! We left after the fireworks, but most stayed until early morning.*

After a few days of relaxing at the compound, John and Vicky took me to the Taj Mahal in Agra, about two hundred kilometres from Delhi. I can only describe the Taj Mahal as majestic! I expected it to be solitary there, but there were many people. Naively, you expect certain things to be a certain way, and most of the time they are not, and then you feel disappointed. But I must say the Taj Mahal was romantic, exactly how I imagined it would be. If I had to use another word to describe the Taj Mahal and its surroundings, it would be elysian.

Elysian? What does that mean? I'll have to Google it... Ah, here it is, Elysian, which means beautiful or creative, divinely inspired, peaceful and perfect.

John and Vicky knew why I was travelling and offered to take me to a Guru they knew who lived outside New Delhi in the mountains. The next day, John took me to his place – a big white building. John introduced me to this Guru and explained what I was trying to achieve by travelling. John told me he would be back later to pick me up.

This building was a solitary retreat where people could come out and spend some quiet time meditating and just being alone. India has very intricate and ancient architecture. It's relatively isolated here, which made me slightly nervous at first, but he soon put me at ease with his calm voice reassuring me that I was not in danger and that nothing terrible would happen to me.

He takes me into a room where all four walls are covered by bookcases full of books, and we sit on these giant bean bags. He asks a young man to bring us some tea. As we sat and got to know each other, I felt more at ease. I elaborated a little more on my situation and the decision I made in the cabin to take time out to travel to uncover my authentic self, who I really was, and what I really wanted. He listened attentively, and he sympathetically nodded as I finished speaking. He explained how he would ask me some questions and give me some advice to help me. He told me that many people come to him to find out who they really are, and what they really want to do in life. And to uncover their talent or gift. To be themselves, not to be someone else. If I had to describe this Guru with one specific word, it would be eunoia, meaning beautiful thinking and a sound mind.

I love it when she uses distinct words to describe something. That's one reason I like reading books; another reason is perhaps that I'm tired of my own story.

He asked me a bunch of questions, one straight after another. The Guru said:

"What are the benefits of travelling? Is it worth it? Do you want what you say you want? Are you willing to

sacrifice something in exchange for that? Are you ready to take the consequences for that? While people travel, they develop a feeling, there's a word for this: hiraeth – a homesickness for a home you can't return to or never was. You are searching for something, but you're not sure what you're searching for. Sometimes people are running away from something, a secret that other people are not supposed to know. However, when we hold secrets, we create shame. Let go of the secrets; you let go of the shame. Travelling has become an enduring and consuming passion. A word describing enduring and consuming passion is aeipathy. While travelling in India, you will discover the beauty in imperfection, and perhaps the acceptance of the cycle of life and death. The beauty in imperfection, the acceptance of the cycle of life and death, is called Wabi-sabi. This concept comes from Japanese wisdom. I will also explain later why the Bhagavad Gita is so special; it encourages us to live with purity, strength, discipline, honesty, kindness, and integrity to find our purpose and live it fully. But before I continue, tell me first a little more about you and your place of work. Then, after that, you can share with me something about your home-life, if you like."

I told him, "For many years now I have worked in a hospital. At times it can be very demanding. I've comprehended as a nurse that it's not just the physical needs that are essential for people, but their emotional needs require attending to, also. Working in the hospital, I have noticed that most of us, if not all of us, have experienced trauma in our childhood. The wound it causes, we try and deal with most of our lives. Some children's emotional needs are not met by their parents. One American doctor, who worked on my ward, told me that the American overdose crisis last year resulted in one hundred thousand deaths. He said to me that it was more than the number of American soldiers that died in the Vietnam, Afghan, and Iraq wars combined. The overdose deaths were called 'death of despair'. If our emotional needs are unmet, we resort to other things to put us in a different state of mind. Sometimes we get addicted to those things. When people are in a state of anomie, suicide rises drastically. Anomie comes from having no meaning – when we have lost all meaning internally and externally.

"I'm not sure about other occupations, but as a nurse or doctor, we encounter a considerable amount of *physical and mental health issues in patients, which takes its toll on us. We see the raw reality of life and of how alarming it can be. Most of us switch off from the stress of our work by watching a movie, or having a glass of wine or two, or going for a run, or doing a hobby. Everyone is just trying to manage life in their own little way. I believe that, as a child, we unconsciously abandon our true selves in the pursuit of safety. We give up our authenticity for attachment because we think if we don't keep the attachment, we won't survive. So, we let authenticity go because we believe people won't like us if we are authentic, if we are being ourselves by listening to our own inner voice, and we end up trying to please people."*

"Okay," the Guru said, "let me start by saying – in childhood, we get influenced by society and the environment we are raised in. In our brain is the Hippocampus; it has recorded all that we have experienced our whole life. What are your three desires? Are they your desires? Or is it what other people expect of you? Environment and certain people influence you starting when you are a child.

"The ego is your enemy; it's against spirituality, and

about perception to be satisfied. Your subconscious programming runs your life which fuels your ego. Try and stay conscious and think consciously as much as possible. When your ego runs your life, you have no power to affect reality.

"Reality is a feedback system that mirrors your beliefs. Self-love is the currency for exchanging thoughts for things you want to achieve. Responsibility – that's where the meaning of life is. What you want to find will be found where you least want to look. Find out where you are in your life and where you want to go. It would be best if you had a goal in life of what you want. Aim for that, then the whole journey will be orientated to get to what you were aiming at. There is a cost of staying where you are, and there is a cost of moving forward. Each moment of our lives is transient; as soon as it happens, it automatically becomes a memory. You never perceive the past as it really was because you see it from your current self-perspective. The present causes the meaning of the past, rather than the past causing the meaning of the present. Whenever you frame a memory, it's from your current self.

"Is life fair? Many people say no, they didn't have the

same opportunities as others. But some people would reply to this comment by saying, knock on the door, and it will be opened. Or ask, and it shall be given. Imagination can be helpful, use it, but use it wisely. Try to be the best version of yourself; it's better for you and the people you come into contact with. Do and say things that empower you and others. When you move forward into the unknown, you move into the realm of infinite possibilities. Words can be perceived differently by all people. Comments can be powerful; choose them wisely so people can identify and feel the same – truly mean them. When people say you didn't spend time together even though you were together the whole time, they mean you did not pay attention to them. The root of the main problem we all have is how we perceive ourselves. (I am not what I think I am. I am not what you think I am. I am, what I think, you think I am.) We live in a perception of a perception of ourselves."

This saying – 'I am' – I recognised straight away from Portugal. Memories flashed back in an instant as soon as I heard this. He continued:

"How you test what you value, is by what you spend your money and time on. It's not what's in your heart or

mind.

"DNA is the repository of memory, of evolution. I look at death as creativity. Every creative process has a death involved. In biology, cells die and then new ones are created. Apoptosis is the definition of this."

I asked the Guru, "Is death final?" This interested me; as a nurse I saw death regularly.

"We will get to this in a moment," he said. "It would be best to concentrate on an idea, ideal, purpose, and meaning in life, not external material things or people. Otherwise, you'll ask yourself: what's it all for? The question is: what is our real identity? Once you discover your real identity beyond space and time, you will realise there is no birth and no death. Just recycling. Just the continuous birth and death as punctual points in the grammar of life. If you awaken who you really are, you won't fear death. If you don't confuse yourself with the role you are playing now as Jane, you are free. If you get attached to the role of Jane, you are in the melodrama of fear and existence. You have forgotten you are like a woman in a cinema watching a movie. You are a witness to the roles you are playing. You are not the roles you play.

"Later, I will explain the Enneagram of Personality, a model of the human psyche that is principally understood and taught as a typology of nine interconnected personality types."

Each time he explained something, he gave me time to reflect on it. Then I asked him what I was always curious about: "What is freedom?"

"Freedom and security are illusions. One of the questions people should ask is: what does your soul want to express?

"Samadhi is the awakening of the dream of your character in the play of life. Samadhi is Sanskrit, – total self-collectedness – and Maya – the illusion of the self. You can only become aware of the soul's purpose when you are able to watch the conditioned self in its endless pursuits and let them go. Life has no inherent meaning; we are the ones who bring meaning to our lives.

"Nobody really likes change; they want to stay in their comfort zone, and something external and internal makes them change or take action."

He continued to explain: "It's essential to understand how your brain contributes to the state of your mind. While most of us focus on looking at our emotions in an attempt to become happier and more spiritual beings, our brainwaves and subconscious also play a key part in our quest for fulfilment."

He told me we would explore the five brainwave frequencies and how they affect our state of mind.

Before he continued, I asked him a question I had been asking myself for some time. "Are we controllers of our reality?"

"We easily forget that we are the controllers of our reality and that 'our reality' is not made up of outside influences, but that it actually consists of our thoughts, beliefs, and mindset. Therefore, by learning about the deeper states of consciousness, you can open your subconscious mind and create your reality at will and with precision. To do this, the first step is understanding your different brain frequencies.

"We all have five – Beta, Alpha, Theta, Delta, and Gamma. Each frequency is measured in cycles per second (Hz) and has its own set of characteristics representing a specific level of brain activity and a unique state of consciousness.

"The first one is Beta – the waking consciousness and reasoning wave.

"Beta brainwaves are associated with normal waking consciousness and a heightened state of alertness, logic, and critical reasoning. While Beta brainwaves are essential for effective functioning throughout the day, they can also translate into stress, anxiety, and restlessness. The voice of Beta can be described as being that nagging little inner critic that gets louder the higher you go into range. Therefore, most adults operate at Beta; it's little surprise that stress is today's most common health problem.

"The second one is Alpha – the deep relaxation wave. Alpha brainwaves are present in deep relaxation, usually when the eyes are closed, when you are slipping into a lovely daydream, or during light meditation. It is an optimal time to program the mind for success, and it also heightens your imagination, visualisation, memory, learning, and concentration. It is the gateway to your subconscious mind and lies at the base of your conscious awareness. The voice of Alpha is your intuition, which becomes clearer and more profound the closer you get to 7.5Hz.

"The third is Theta – the light meditation and sleeping wave. Theta brainwaves are present during light

meditation and light sleep, including the all-important REM dream state. It is the realm of your subconsciousness and is only experienced momentarily as you drift off to sleep from Alpha and wake from deep sleep (Delta). It is said that a sense of deep spiritual connection and unity with the universe can be experienced at Theta. Your mind's most deep-seated programs are at Theta, and it is where you experience vivid visualisations, great inspiration, profound creativity, and exceptional insight. Unlike your other brainwaves, the elusive voice of Theta is a silent voice. It is at the Alpha-Theta border, from 7Hz to 8Hz, where the optimal range for visualisation, mind programming, and using the creative power of your mind begins. It's the mental state in which you consciously create your reality. At this frequency, you are conscious of your surroundings; however, your body is in deep relaxation.

"The fourth is Delta, which is the deep sleep wave. The Delta frequency is the slowest of the frequencies and is experienced in deep, dreamless sleep and in very deep, transcendental meditation where awareness is fully detached. Delta is the realm of your unconscious mind, and the gateway to the universal mind and the collective

unconsciousness, where information received is otherwise unavailable at the conscious level.

"Among many things, deep sleep is important for the healing process, as it's linked with deep healing and regeneration. Hence, not having enough deep sleep is detrimental to your health in more ways than one.

"And the fifth is Gamma – the insight wave. This range is the most recently discovered and is the fastest frequency at above 40Hz. While little is known about this state of mind, initial research shows Gamma waves are associated with bursts of insight and high–level information processing.

"People have to have some aspiration, ambition, goal, objective, aim, desire, or wish in order to have a reference point as to where to start. What was your aspiration before you left Canada to embark on your trip?"

I had to think before elaborating on my aspiration, but my mind went blank. Then I blurted out: "To find me, that little girl from many years ago that used to be me. Over the years, I've drifted so far apart from her."

"If you go into nature or somewhere quiet and start meditating regularly, you will eventually become aware of who you really are and what your purpose is here, giving you meaning in your life. To be fully alive, you must experience each moment as completely new and fresh. To live is to be willing to die over and over again."

We sat there in silence for what seemed like ages, and then he carried on talking.

"John told me you like to hear or read philosophical quotes. I would like to share some excerpts from well-known people if that's okay; maybe you have heard of them before, and maybe not.

"Einstein once said, 'The true measure of a human being is determined primarily by the measure and sense which is attained in liberation from the self.'

"Joseph Campbell said, 'Your life is the fruit of your own doing; you have no one to blame but yourself.' He also said, 'We must be willing to get off the life we've planned to have the life that is waiting for us.' Another was, 'The privilege of a lifetime is being who you are.'"

I liked them; I hadn't heard of those ones before. I will definitely take his advice and meditate in nature or a quiet place as frequently as possible.

Interesting, I'm beginning to like hearing these quotes. I'm starting to understand myself more. I'm becoming more consciously aware that as an introvert my strengths are deep thinking, productivity in solitude, and creativity in expressing myself when needed. My observation skills are acute; I notice a lot and have an eye for detail. By being creative when painting, singing, making pottery, etc., I believe you are experiencing your soul, the real you. The relationship I have with certain people is deep. I put a worth on my autonomy and independence. Our sovereignty and autonomy are essential, and it's a paradox because supposedly we are all connected.

The Guru suggested I go outside and sit in the quietness of the garden and be aware of what thoughts come to me. As I sat there, I thought of the power that belief, fear, and love can have to determine the course of our lives. Yesterday the course of my life was heading in one direction, and today it is heading in another. Each encounter with a person or experience is a crossroads where we have to make a decision – a choice – which puts us on another trajectory. Different stages of our life are like mini lives – in each stage is a different you.

John arrived to pick me up, so I said goodbye to the Guru and thanked him for his wisdom and insight. He has helped me enormously to come one step further in my pursuit of discovering my true authentic self. But before I left, the Guru gave me one more piece of advice. He told me many people try and find the right door in life, but you will waste a lot of time doing this if you don't have the right key. So, remember, it's all about having the right key.

Chapter Six

Nepal

'The measure of intelligence is the ability to change.'

- Albert Einstein -

March

The flight from India to Tribhuvan International Airport in Kathmandu, Nepal, takes one hour and fifty minutes. Bhim, my husband's former colleague who worked with him in Doha, Qatar, will be at the airport to pick me up. Apparently, he has his own security company now. As I sit on the plane, anxious thoughts go through my head. I hope my baggage got loaded on this plane and not another. I'm constantly worried that my luggage will get lost.

Bhim was waiting at arrivals; he was a polite, quiet-mannered guy. He greeted me with, "Namaste." We made our way out of the airport, walked to the car park where his four-by-four jeep was parked, and loaded my baggage onto the back seat. We drove approximately thirty minutes into downtown Thamel. He had to pick something up for his wife before we carried on to his home, which is situated just on the outskirts. As I looked outside the car window, I could see rickshaws, the dense traffic of vehicles erratically swerving in and out to overtake each other, and the honking of horns that were reminiscent of India.

Shirisha, his wife, and their son, Bhabish, greeted me at the front door of their house. Shirisha used to be an air stewardess before they had Bhabish. She still looked very glamorous. She had prepared a typical Nepalese meal for me; it looked and smelt delicious. It consisted of rice, a thick lentil soup, a curry of vegetables, and spicy vegetables macerated in vinegar. After unpacking some of my things in their spare bedroom and getting a quick wash, I went downstairs to drink tea with them. As the flight was not long, Shirisha suggested that she and Bhim take me to downtown Thamel to look around. It was about a twenty minute drive, and I noticed many small and differently coloured flags draped up across the roads everywhere.

Bhim explained to me that they represent prayers. There are many temples in and around Kathmandu; it seems very spiritual here. Shirisha told me that the religion in Nepal is eighty percent Hindu, ten percent Buddhist, and ten percent other religions. We managed to find a small kiosk where I could exchange some money for the Nepalese Rupee to buy a few souvenirs. The Thamel area is very touristic, with many tiny shops selling backpacks, tents, sleeping bags, boots and jackets for hiking in the mountains. That night we stayed up reasonably late discussing a variety of subjects. Bhim was interested in various things from UFOs, to extra-terrestrials, to the paranormal, and to past lives; he was curious about anything mysterious.

My circadian rhythm has become out of sync from travelling over the last months, and even though the discussion was fascinating, I was desperate to get to bed. They said they would take me up into the mountains tomorrow and visit a relative who owns a hotel called Hotel At The End Of The Universe, and that we could have lunch there. I wished them a good night and told them I was looking forward to our excursion the next day.

As I lay in bed, my mind began to wander. Next month will be Easter; being away and missing events back in Canada has made me homesick.

Time is a significant factor in our lives. Many people

would like things to stay the same, to never change. The most valuable thing you have in your life is your time and energy, and both are limited. We attempt to change reality because it doesn't suit us and doesn't fit our expectations. We try and change reality to fit our own desires. We struggle to change external events or people, but what we should actually do is change ourselves from within, our thoughts and perspectives.

Time stands still for nobody. People evolve; nothing stays the same. There is one thing in the world that is constant, and that is change. People would like things or other people to remain the same – familiar, the status quo. But it's just a matter of time, and change is inevitable. At night when it is silent, I sometimes have emotions that surface. Most people are afraid of silence or being alone in their own company. However, sometimes it can be calming or therapeutic. I'm beginning to doubt if I should carry on with my journey. Even though I've met some interesting people and seen some incredible sights, I miss Canada and my friends and family. Being away for such a long period has made me feel like I'm missing out on something. However, I'm at the point of no return. I've managed to get this far. I can't give up now, otherwise it would have been in vain.

Even though I'm tired, I can't get to sleep, so I read a little. Just as I want to put my book down and get some sleep, I notice a perfect quote for inserting into my journal:

'It is never too late to be who you might have been.'
George Eliot.

The next day we drove up into the mountains. On the way, we stopped to get out, stretch our legs, and walk a little. Being quiet, not hearing the noise of traffic, the masses of people talking, etc., is soothing to the soul. It also lets in answers which you have been asking yourself. The busyness of life makes time fly by. When you take the time to be still in quietness, you have time to reflect, introspect, and sometimes even enjoy and be grateful for certain things in your life. It's being in homeostasis when you can eventually be in quietness and quiet your mind of thoughts. Silence at first can be scary, but it can be a good friend after a while. It slowly makes you become a good friend to yourself. You stop being so hard on yourself over a selection of circumstances. You interact with life differently when you have come to peace with yourself. We are the one who brings meaning to our lives.

We eventually reached the hotel and had a lovely lunch in the restaurant. The setting brought up cultural differences and issues of not offending. The panoramic view from the bay window of the restaurant of the mountain range surrounding us was spectacular! Literally breath-taking! After lunch, we sat there over a flavoursome Nepalese cup of coffee and discussed my journey's next stage: China. Bhim brought up the subject of digital currency, which is starting to be used in China, and that perhaps other countries will be phasing out fiat currency, which would be a shame as I like the uniqueness of these various currencies, which is a part of their distinctive identity. Also, traditions in many countries define them, make them attractive, and are obviously part of their history. He also mentioned the number of people in the world today compared to just sixty years ago. In 1960 there were three billion people, and the population now is at 7.8 billion. This has had an effect on natural resources. He also said that the younger generation will probably have to change their career three or four times in their lifetime to keep up with the evolution of the ever-changing world.

Mmm, it seems as though I will have to reinvent

myself many times throughout my life to stay in work.

Usually, you feel vulnerable as a small minority in a strange country, and venturing into the unknown makes you feel powerless. However, having Bhim and Shirisha with me makes me feel secure in their presence.

Shirisha questioned me if I knew what Samadhi was.

I answered her with, "Samadhi is the awakening of the dream of your character in the play of life."

She smiled and asked me, "What about Maya?"

I told her, "Maya is the illusion of the self."

She said, "Wow, you have certainly done your homework; I'm impressed."

Of course, I only knew this as I had recently been told it in India.

We went on to Pashupatinath Temple; this temple is known for those who cremate their dead and mourn in full view of locals and tourists. In Hinduism, this is the task of the eldest son. Bhim told me that when his father died, he also had to prepare the plinth where his body would be cremated. On the way back to their home, we stopped off at a couple of small villages so I could take some photos of the magnificent Temples. Shirisha said she would like to take me to visit her parents tomorrow, and, after that, we'll meet up with a couple of her friends and go for a coffee at her favourite café. When we got back, I had to excuse myself and told them I felt tired and had to go to bed earlier if I was going to have a full day tomorrow seeing her parents and friends.

I heard packs of wild dogs fighting with one another late at night as they roam the streets, keeping me from getting quality sleep, which I desperately need. The next day, as it has become my ritual, I bought the Kathmandu Post newspaper to read about what is happening locally. I received a text from a friend who informs me that my so-called best friend frequently visits my husband at the house, bringing him meals she has prepared, and sometimes cooking at our home. I've tried phoning her, but she's not answering. I'll send her a text later asking what she's up to. I know how she is, always going after men, but I never thought she would try it with my husband. I don't trust her; she has a hidden agenda, I'm sure of it. I have all sorts of thoughts going through my head, now. I have to try and calm down, but being so far away and unable to take action is difficult. I feel helpless that I'm not in control of the circumstances at home. I feel angry. The secondary feeling, the underlying feeling I have, is powerlessness.

In the morning, Shirisha asked me if we could go to the café first before visiting her parents and meeting up with her friends; she wanted to ask my advice on something.

While we were drinking our coffee, she told me she had asked family members and friends what they thought if Bhim, her, and Bhabish decided to immigrate to America. She has a cousin there who has told her how good it is. Shirisha said her friends and family don't want them to leave Nepal, but she said Bhim and her are still young, and if they don't take this opportunity to go now, they might not have another chance again. If they had another opportunity later, they might be too old. She said the advice I would give her would be an objective view; that's why she asked me. She hesitated for a moment and wanted to ask me something but then decided not to. I intuitively knew something was bothering her, and my motherly instinct was to hug her and ask what the matter was, but I didn't. I felt myself being put in a difficult position; whatever influence I had on this young lady would have consequences. I would have to be careful in what I say to her. However, I sensed she seemed confused about how to go on with her life, and she was desperately reaching out to me for assistance. I told her I had something that might help her. I groped around in my bag until I found my notebook, in which, over the years as a nurse, I wrote down various things that patients had told me that I felt were important to remember. I told her these were comments from mostly elderly patients I was nursing in the hospital and asked her if I could read them to her, hoping some of them would help guide her and give her the direction that she was so obviously seeking. With a sigh of relief, she immediately agreed and listened attentively.

I just started to read them out in no specific order, hoping that at least a couple of them would benefit her:

"To not travel when you have the chance. Travelling becomes infinitely more complex the older you get, especially if you have a family and need to pay the way for three-plus people instead of just yourself. Not learning another language. You'll kick yourself when you realise you took three years of language in high school and remember none of it. Staying in a bad relationship. No one who ever gets out of a bad relationship looks back without wishing they had made a move sooner.

Regret missing the chance to see your favourite bands. Being scared to do things.

"Looking back, you'll think: what was I so afraid of? Failing to make physical fitness a priority. Too many of us spend the physical peak of our lives on the couch. When you hit forty, fifty, sixty, and beyond, you'll dream of what you could have done. Letting yourself be defined by gender roles. Few things are as sad as an old person saying, "Well, it just wasn't done back then." Not quitting a terrible job. Look, you have got to pay the bills. But if you don't make a plan to improve your situation, you might wake up one day having spent forty years in hell. Not trying harder in school. It's not just that your grades play a role in determining where you end up in life. Eventually, you'll realise how neat it was to spend all day learning and wish you had paid more attention. Not realising how beautiful you were. Too many of us spend our youth unhappy with the way we look, but the reality is that's when we're our most beautiful.

"Being afraid to say, "I love you." When you're old, you won't care if your love wasn't returned – only that you made it known how you felt. Not listening to your parents' advice. You don't want to hear it when you're

young, but the infuriating truth is that most of what your parents say about life is true. Caring too much about what other people think. In twenty years, you won't care about any of those people you once worried so much about. Supporting other people's dreams over your own. Supporting others is a beautiful thing, but not when it means you never get to shine. Not moving on fast enough. Old people look back at the long periods spent picking themselves off the ground from conflict experiences as nothing but wasted time. Holding grudges, especially with those you love. What's the point of re-living the anger over and over?

"Not standing up for yourself. Old people don't take nonsense from anyone, and neither should you. Not volunteering enough – nearing the end of one's life without having helped to make the world a better place is a source of sadness for many. Neglecting your teeth. Brush, floss, and get regular check-ups. It will all seem so maddeningly easy when you have dentures. Missing the chance to ask your grandparents questions before they die. Most of us realise too late what an awesome resource grandparents are. They can explain everything you'll ever wonder about where you came from, but only

if you ask them in time.

"Working too much. No one looks back from their deathbed and wishes they spent more time at the office, but they wish they spent more time with family, friends, and doing hobbies. Not learning how to cook one incredible meal – knowing one drool-worthy meal will make all those dinner parties and celebrations special. Not stopping enough to appreciate the moment. Young people are constantly on the go, but stopping to take it all in now and again is a good thing. Failing to finish what you start. "I had big dreams of becoming a counsellor. I even signed up for the classes, but then..." Refusing to let friendships run their course – people grow apart.

"Clinging to what was, instead of acknowledging that things have changed, can be a source of ongoing agitation and sadness. Not playing with your kids enough. When you're old, you'll realise your kid went from wanting to play with you to wanting you out of their room in the blink of an eye. Never taking a significant risk (especially in love). Knowing that you took a leap of faith at least once, even if you fell flat on your face, will be a great comfort when you're old. Not taking the time to develop contacts and networks. Networking may seem

like a bunch of crap when you're young, but it becomes clear how so many jobs are won later on. Worrying too much. Most things we worry about never happen anyway. Getting caught up in the needless drama. Who needs it? Not spending enough time with loved ones. Our time with our loved ones is finite. Make it count. Never performing in front of others. This isn't a regret for everyone, but many elderly people wish they knew, just once, what it was like to stand in front of a crowd and show off their talents. Not being grateful sooner. It can be hard to see initially, but eventually it becomes clear that every moment on this earth, from the mundane to the amazing, is a gift that we're all fortunate to share.

"Love your life. Take pictures of everything. Tell people you love them. Talk to random strangers. Do things that you're scared to do. So many of us die, and no one remembers a thing we did. Take your life and make it the best story in the world. Don't waste it.

"If you could come back again, what would you be: a man or a woman? Are you happy with the life you have now? Are you glad you had the parents you have now? Are you satisfied with where you live? What would you be in your next life? A baker, or a driver, perhaps? What if?

What if you could come back and re-live life again; what would you do differently? But what is it that you are supposed to do? You have to look inward and ask yourself truthfully what you desire.

"Friends, one day, will get separated from each other. We will miss our conversations. Days, months, and years will pass until our contact becomes rare. One day, our children will see our photos and ask: "Who are these people?" and we will smile with invisible tears and say, "It was with them that I had the best days of my life."

Shirisha sat silently for a short time to digest what I had just read to her. She thanked me and told me she had a lot to think about before she and Bhim would make a decision. I could see throughout the day that she was trying to process everything I'd read to her. Shirisha said it's like an inner dialogue, a committee going on inside her head all the time, all the voices in her head working against each other. She said she tries to quiet them to listen to her true self, her intuition.

Life pushes back when you're not supposed to encounter certain things at that specific time. Perhaps return at a later date when the circumstances are right for you.

After reading this journal segment, I question my real identity. My parents expected me to be a certain way, and my teachers and the kids at school expected me to be a specific image; when I didn't conform to these expectations, they couldn't connect with me the way they wanted. They were annoyed because they could not control how they wanted me to act.

This section in the journal has made me aware of all the anguish I've endured over the years; it appears I've disassociated from myself, and I need to find myself and connect again.

The last couple of years I have felt alone amongst many people in a crowd, and I was becoming a hermit. Mr. Kamanski, the school counsellor, told me I couldn't live as an island. He said people need their fellow man; to see themselves as a reflection of their fellow man. I think you can feel lonely anywhere in the world. Mr. Kamanski said that it's your state of mind which determines loneliness. I have felt loneliness as an emptiness that is frightening and scary. This empty dark void. Loneliness is about feeling lost, and you want to find direction and search for something. You are uncertain what that something is or should be. My opinion is that depression and loneliness go hand in hand. Life is about reality – there is no shortcut. I know intellectually what is right and wrong in life, but I still get melancholic. I wish I could be happier. I try and force myself sometimes, but it doesn't work.

I used to think: what's the sense of all this? Why torture myself for years, being unable to be happy when we will all eventually die anyway? Why don't I just put myself out of my misery now?

But, reading Jane's journal has inspired me to try and look at things with a different mindset.

Last night, the whole house shook; we all came out of our bedrooms to see why. It was very frightening, and Bhim said we'd had a minor earthquake.

This morning, we heard there wasn't too much damage from the earthquake. However, we were informed we would get aftershocks. Bhim suggested that it would probably be best if I got a flight out of Nepal as quickly as possible in case the aftershocks damaged the airport, as I would have difficulty leaving Nepal. So, I packed my bags and said my goodbyes to Shirisha and Bhabish, and then Bhim drove me to the airport. Many tourists were there trying to get on the next available flight out of Nepal, and Bhim said he would stay with me until he knew I could definitely board my flight to China.

As I sit at departures waiting for confirmation that I can board my flight, Bhim is busy discussing the damage from the earthquake with some airport staff. I read my book to pass the time and find a quote to insert into my journal:

'Never lose the moon while counting the stars. At some point, we will look back at our past and realise that we cared too much about things that don't matter. No one is always busy. It is just a matter of priorities. No matter how busy you are, show love for those who have always been there for you. Some of them might not be there for long. Appreciate what you have and who you have because the future can take them all away from you anytime. Do it before it is too late. Say it before you run out of time. Love is about mutual appreciation and admiration. It does not require something in return. Only from the heart can you touch the sky.' Rumi.

That quote by Rumi prompted me to look on my phone at the photos I keep there of my family and friends. Of happy times of everyone enjoying themselves. Oh, how young we all look there. I can't believe the style of clothes we used wear, and our hairstyles... well, no comment. Does our past depict our future, how we are now? When I looked at the photos from when I was younger, I knew it was me but a different version. Am I still the same person? I was always a perfectionist, and keeping that up for so long has become stressful. I ask myself: when I dig deep down into the abyss of myself, what have I learnt from this journey? What have I been able to bring to my awareness of what I've learnt throughout my life? I answered myself with – the meaning of life is the experience of life. We think the meaning of life is getting what we want and avoiding what we don't want. When we ask ourselves, "What do I want?" we mention a few things, but that's not what we genuinely want. We might say we want a relationship, a car, or a house, but the caveat is you will eventually be unfulfilled. It's not true that we want these things. What we really want is to feel good inside, to feel love, joy, happiness, satisfaction, and meaning. For most of our lives, we chase after external things that we think will make us happy. For the other part of our lives, we try to avoid the things we don't want. It's in our mind that we think things make us happy or not.

They are calling us to the check-in to start boarding; I have to give Bhim a hug and say goodbye. But before I do, I have to include one last quote:

'Everyone has oceans to fly, if they have the heart to do it. Is it reckless? Maybe. But what do dreams know of boundaries?' Amelia Earhart.

Chapter Seven

China

'If you don't want to obey others, you will have to learn to obey yourself. That is not as easy as it sounds.'

- Fredrich Nietzsche -

April

The flight from Kathmandu, Nepal, to Chengdu, China, takes two hours and fifty minutes. I used the time on the flight to read up specifically on Chengdu and the surrounding area in China, which Bhim was kind enough to print off at his place of work for me. My husband had prearranged for a guy called James to meet me at Chengdu Shangliu International Airport. He was a Chinese guy my husband worked with for a short time in London, procuring parts for a Palm Oil mill in Nigeria. He works in London for approximately eight months of the year, then returns to China to be with his family for four months. His English is very impressive. However, China has advanced dramatically over the last few years, so he's seriously considering staying in China to work now. I will stay with him, his wife, and his new-born baby daughter for a few days until he can find a suitable hotel for me to check into.

The next day James' wife, Xiu-Xiu, and I took a walk around where they lived while he looked after their baby daughter. Everybody is living in high-story apartments. I don't see any houses; perhaps there are houses on the outskirts. She took me to a small tea house just around the corner to sit and talk. She told me that in China, the population is 1.4 billion. The language is mainly Mandarin. Chengdu is the birthplace of Chinese tea culture, and Chengdu has more teahouses than any other city in the world. I asked her for the short duration I would stay in Chengdu if she could teach me a little Mandarin. She agreed and asked if I was interested in teaching young children English for an hour or so each day, as many parents are searching for English-speaking people to teach their children English. I said I would love to. This would be a perfect way to immerse myself in their community and interact with the people. While drinking our tea, she telephoned a few of her friends to come and introduce themselves to me. Most of her friends could not speak English like Xiu-Xiu or James, and she had to translate everything I said. I also noticed there were absolutely no signs in English anywhere. I became very quickly aware this would be the first time for me where I would have significant problems with communication.

For lunch, we had Peking duck. She paid by her mobile phone in digital currency. She informed me that not everywhere in China uses digital or cryptocurrency; there are still places using the Renminbi. She told me there has been an unprecedented change from old China to new China, moving at an accelerated pace over the last decade. Not just the Chinese are finding it challenging to keep up with the accelerating growth, but also the rest of the world. Xiu-Xiu told me most companies have a slogan, and it goes like this: 'Sell the problem you solve – not the product!'

Xiu-Xiu and I take a taxi to the Chengdu town centre. China has been a big wake-up call for me on how this country has evolved so rapidly! How modern the world is becoming with fast-paced technology and social media. Chinese people think and work towards the future, not staying stuck in the past like other countries. However, I believe people in the West are not as personal as before; they have become impersonal. Empathy towards other people is getting less. Since I started travelling, I have enjoyed exploring; I'm becoming more curious about many things and learning new insights into how people go about their daily lives. Surprisingly, they are very similar to people back in Canada. I suppose it's naive of me to think otherwise. People go to work to pay for their mortgage or rented accommodation, children go to school, parents spend time with their children and grandchildren, watch TV, etc. But, of course, the culture is slightly different; some have different religions, beliefs, languages, and monetary systems. Some are more materialistic, and others are more spiritual. But that's what makes travelling so enjoyable, seeing and experiencing all the unique things about that country. The way they dress, the specific food they eat, their idiosyncrasies. I find it fascinating; I've found most people are sociable and accepting of foreigners coming into their country. This was one of my fears when I started off on my journey, to be met with hostility towards me. Even after hearing all the positive stories from my husband about his travels, I still had trepidation. My view of the world has significantly changed over the last six months.

China has three major religious traditions – Taoism, Confucianism, and Buddhism. Taoism or Daoism is pronounced both ways. I see the Yin and Yang symbol – feminine and masculine – on some car windows. Somehow it reminded me of the drawings and paintings my daughter used to do when she was a child. Xiu-Xiu has been reading a book that her husband James brought back from London for her; it's called Ikigai. *It's a Japanese philosophy of finding purpose. She has another book she has just finished reading, which James brought back for her last year. It's the Chinese philosophy* Tae Te Ching *by Lau Tzu. She told me that the first page starts with, 'At the centre of your being, you have the answer; you know who you are and know what you want.' I thought to myself, "That's the book for me! Where can I buy a copy? Ha-ha!"*

We left the town centre and headed towards the outskirts of Chengdu. There, Xiu-Xiu took me to a sanctuary where Panda bears are kept. After that, we drove up into the surrounding mountainous hills, where I eventually saw some houses and not high-story buildings. The people there live a simple life, but they seem happy enough. On the way back to Xiu-Xiu's place it was getting dark, and I could see the lights on in all the skyscrapers; it was quite overwhelming, being surrounded by so many buildings. I just wasn't used to it.

The next day I thought I would try and go out by myself. Xiu-Xiu wrote down her address to keep with me so I could show a taxi driver to get me back to hers. She also told me what bus number to get if I wanted to go into town. Eventually, I bought a bus ticket using a lot of hand signs to try and be understood and some Chinese words that Xiu-Xiu taught me. After a few of stops, I had to change to the metro, which some young girl who could speak a little English told me I had to do. However, I got off two stops earlier than I should have because I didn't understand what was said on the intercom. All the signs were in Chinese at the station, and all the people I was asking for directions to the town couldn't speak English. Of course, I had miss-placed the piece of paper with Xiu-Xiu's address which I could have given to a taxi driver. I started to panic; this was the first time I was terrified and completely out of my comfort zone.

I could at least converse in English with the people in other countries I had visited. I felt utterly isolated and helpless here. My anxiety was rising; I couldn't think *properly. This was what I was constantly fearing would happen to me. I couldn't phone Xiu-Xiu as I left my phone at her place. I'm always forgetting things and not paying attention. My husband always got annoyed with me for doing this. I sat on the station platform bench and tried to calm myself down so I could think coherently. I felt like everything was closing in on me. Because I thought I handled everything so well in other countries, I got overconfident, thinking I could handle it here. I was wrong! What was I thinking of coming on such a trip by myself? I feel so insecure and out of my depth here; I don't really belong. I'm lonely and want to go back home to Canada. Tears were welling up in my eyes; I tilted my head slightly downwards so nobody would notice my state. Like a bolt of lightning, I remembered what Charles said about what happened to my husband in Abu Dhabi when he wasn't aware of where he was and had to check into a hotel.*

How terrified he must have felt. I can definitely sympathise now with what he must have been going through. Then I noticed a mother with her small daughter holding her hand standing in front of me. She was saying something to me, but I didn't understand her as she spoke

Chinese. Then she mentioned Xiu-Xiu's name, and I recognised she was one of the women I met in the tea house. The little girl asked me in broken English if I was okay, and I said yes, but I needed to return to Xiu-Xiu's apartment. The little girl spoke to her mother, and the woman smiled, put her hand in mine, and said something in Chinese. The little girl looked at me with a big smile and said, "We take you." I found out later that the little girl had been taking private English lessons at home.

As Friedrich Nietzsche once said, 'You are never destroyed by anyone except yourself.'

It seems as though her internal conflict is desire clashing with fear! Fear is what keeps her from not taking action. This incident jogged my memory from my psychology classes at school when we learned about situational awareness – the ability to absorb and process meaningful information about our current environment. Also, compartmentalisation – the ability to effectively chunk an environment or situation into significant pieces and then focus on that which needs immediate attention. She has sensory overload in China, which is too much for her.

I wouldn't be surprised if Jane tried to retreat and

return to her life as it was. I think this could be the turning point where she might give up. I hope not; she's done so well to get this far. She has inspired me so much up until now.

I found out from my husband today that my best friend who was going around to my house has cancer. She has been speaking to my husband to get moral support. She didn't inform me because she didn't want me to break off with my travels. She told my husband she would talk with me when I return to Canada. The cancer is in the process of getting taken care of. She learnt she had cancer just before I left Canada, but didn't tell me as she knew I would put her before myself by staying and trying to help. I thought of breaking off my journey and returning to Canada. Still, after much deliberation with my husband, I decided to remain in China and teach children English for the duration I have left here. Xiu-Xiu explained that perhaps I have come to the end of my nursing career, and that I should consider taking up a second career in teaching, perhaps in Canada, to foreign pupils. This would be called using my 'crystallised intelligence'. She said 'fluid intelligence' is one's ability to process new information, learn, and solve problems, and 'crystallised intelligence' is one's stored knowledge accumulated over the years. She thinks I feel redundant to a certain extent, because my daughter has grown up and is flourishing as a young adult and doesn't need to depend on her mother so much now but on her fiancé. She thinks I feel a sense of loss, that I'm not needed anymore. I sadly have to admit I agree with everything she said.

And, regarding changing my career, I've thought I might become a counsellor when I return to Canada. Finding meaning in your job is essential; meaning is not about the what but the why.

Xiu-Xiu said part of my life's purpose was to care for my daughter. However, I have to adapt to my daughter being an adult now, and I have to treat her in this manner, not as a young child.

That's right; by the sound of things, Jane has cared for patients and her family for many years and has not paid attention to her own needs. I get the impression that in China she feels as though she is isolated and feels so lonely. Everything seems to be closing in on her. I sense this is the lowest ebb she has reached on her travels; she hasn't felt this low since she left Canada. I presume that has been the problem with Jane all the years. She has neglected her inner voice of what she wanted to do because Jane always ensured other people were okay, even though it seems to me Jane often received no appreciation for everything she did. Her subconscious or her inner child is saying: enough is enough. She needs and longs to revert to her old self and return to Canada, but she knows she will betray herself if she does this. I bet back in her childhood she would always try and please her parents, but Jane would never get recognition for anything she did. I think Jane realises she has been doing this her whole life with almost everybody she meets. Jane knows she must stop this behaviour of seeking recognition and appreciation from others, be satisfied and content with herself, and not be code dependent on other people's opinions. Since Jane has been travelling, she has noticed that you don't actually know what you want if you don't know yourself. Then you are caught between two situations; security, which can become boring, and excitement, which can become addictive. You have to align with who you authentically are and what you genuinely want. I think Jane and I are similar; we're afraid of being honest with ourselves and discovering something about ourselves that we don't want to.

I received seven small brown envelopes from my best friend before I left Canada and was instructed not to open any until I was halfway through my journey. In each of the envelopes was a list of seven questions. In the first envelope, which I opened today, the seven questions were:

Why do we all fear death? Is time only a concept made by humans? Is it something we restrict ourselves to? What are we holding on so tightly to that we must let go of? Who is writing the story of our life? When our children reach adulthood, do we want them to be successful, rich, or happy? Why do we need validation so much?

It seemed my friend wanted me to find out the answers to these questions while I was travelling, either to help me or to tell her. Perhaps both – she didn't say.

One thing I have learnt since travelling is: everyone experiences pain, and most suffer from patterns that continue to make life miserable unless something or someone intervenes. The pain we feel comes from the energies that keep curving back and cancelling the wise self and the good word that waits to be expressed from within us. Persistent pain is usually the indication that we have become trapped in a life too small for our true nature. That is the usual human fate and the common predicament where the little-self obscures the greater nature behind it. Until people realise what harms limits them from within, they are unlikely to call out for someone to help stop the pain. The remedy might be nearby, but until the pain becomes unbearable, most remain caught in the agony of self-inflicted wounds. As Rumi says, 'The cure for pain is in the pain.'

I have realised another thing that Anais Nin describes perfectly for me: 'The secret of a full life is to live and relate to others as if they might not be there tomorrow. It eliminates the vice of procrastination, the sin of postponement, failed communications, and failed communions. This thought has made me more and more attentive to all encounters, meetings, and introductions, which might contain the seed of depth that might be carelessly overlooked. This feeling has become a rarity and rarer every day now that we have reached a hastier and more superficial rhythm, now that we believe we are in touch with a more significant amount of people and more countries. This illusion might cheat us of being in touch deeply with the one breathing next to us. The dangerous time when mechanical voices, radios, and telephones, take the place of human intimacies, and the concept of being in touch with millions brings greater and greater poverty in intimacy and human vision.'

I have also become aware that it is only when you meet someone of a different culture from yourself that you begin to realise your beliefs. Sometimes a good story will remind you of who you want to be, good and evil, the triumph of the human spirit, stories about living and dying, and how you have to do one despite the other. I have found that we should speak so that others love to listen to us. And we should listen so that others love to talk to us.

Also, your diet is not only what you eat. It is what you watch, what you listen to, what you read, and the people you hang around. Pay attention to what you feed your soul, not just your stomach.

I have concluded that society has reached the point where everybody has a right, but nobody has a responsibility.

I have also learnt that fasting (when done correctly and for the right reasons) does something to you that *cannot be explained with human language. You become very aware of just how habitual the act of eating has become. Many of us do not eat for hunger; we eat for pleasure. The absence of perpetual pleasure-seeking (in all forms) exposes you to the emotions you mask with your habits, and you are finally exposed to who you indeed are. This is where the healing starts. Physically, emotionally, and spiritually.*

The universe will keep sending us experiences to get our attention until we accept our life and full responsibility. Many people gripe about not getting what they want, such as: a chance, a relationship, or a job. Nobody owes us anything. Most people don't care about our personal circumstances. Only about what we can do for them.

One major thing I've noticed since being in China is how advanced they have become with technology, and I ask myself, do we control our own technology, or is it directing us?

The first Chinese child I taught English to today was the child from the lady who brought me back to Xiu-Xiu's apartment that dreaded day when I had a meltdown on the train station platform. It was my way of saying thank you for her helping me. As I was sitting there and teaching this small child, I had a flashback of my mother teaching me various things when I was a child. I suddenly realised that my mother had so much patience with me while she was teaching me specific things. It never really dawned on me until today. How strange; how was I not aware of that until today?

That's weird; I was thinking about my mother and what she said to my father when I was a young girl. "Raising children is like gardening – nurture them and be patient." I also remember one night, while lying in my bed as a young girl, I could hear my mother saying to my father, "Loving another human being also means that you want what's best for them, even if that means they end up with someone else. You either grow together or grow apart. It's simple but never that easy. Love is so much more than feelings." When I reflect on that now, it seems that perhaps my dad was thinking of leaving my mom for someone else.

Then I remember my dad saying, "I don't want my daughter being treated how my parents treated me as a child." Peculiar that I think of that now. Perhaps all this reading is stirring up some past memories. It's also made me re-evaluate my current state of affairs; I need to figure out how to live the rest of my life. I used to love reading, sometimes probably for escapism, and I used to write poetry, too. During those times, I didn't want to be seen. So much of our life is motivated to be seen. People wish for the feeling of being seen and noticed. Maybe I can become a writer? I can imagine some people I know asking: why do you want to write for a living? My answer would be that we get to expose the truth that others cannot see. And sometimes, we get to change a broken world with our words.

I have to say, my time in China I can only describe for me as being a solitary experience. Nobody has mistreated me, but I feel so lonely. I've never felt so vulnerable as here, probably because I couldn't make myself understood by the local people. Perhaps if I stayed longer, I could adapt better. However, I still enjoyed being with Xiu-Xiu on the outskirts of Chengdu. As I walked around some of the back streets, elderly people were seated at a table on the sidewalk playing a board game called mojo, and children played in front of the small shops. It was a calm and relaxed feeling in the air. I must admit, those times I enjoyed.

I must pack my bags again for the next stage of my adventure to Thailand, Malaysia, and Singapore. The last week I haven't done anything except rest to ensure I have enough energy for the travelling ahead of me. I said my goodbyes to Xiu-Xiu and thanked her for looking after me while staying in her country.

James took me to the airport. Before I went through to departures, James gave me a book as a small gift to read on my travels, which he bought last time he was in London, England. It was by James Green, based on a true story, and he said I would find it interesting.

In the departure lounge, I write one last quote in my journal before I board the plane:

'Until you spread your wings, you'll have no idea how far you can fly.' Napoleon Bonaparte.

Chapter Eight

Thailand – Malaysia – Singapore – part one

'Nowhere can I think so happily as in a train.'

- A.A. Milne -

April-May

After seven hours and forty minutes, I arrived at Suvarnabhumi International Airport in Bangkok. I wouldn't like to try and pronounce that airport's name after a few alcoholic beverages. My husband doesn't know anybody here who can greet me at the airport and assist me in any way, so I have to get a taxi to my hotel, which is, thank goodness, not that far away. Fortunately, I utilised the last week in China to book all the arrangements regarding the hotels and the train I would use to travel from Thailand through Malaysia down to Singapore. During this part of the journey, I will have nobody to help me in any of the countries, and I will have to rely entirely on my wits and intelligence. Which should be interesting...

The train from Thailand through Malaysia to Singapore is approximately two thousand kilometres long. Thailand and Malaysia are third-world countries, whereas Singapore is a modern, developed country. As I sit in my hotel room, I open the second envelope from my best friend. The seven questions are:

Why does the concept of power thrill people so much? Why do we feel the need to control everything? How often do you tell people you love them? Would you have rather tried and failed than not try at all? What was the last thing you spent on that felt genuinely worth it? What was the most significant thing you did in the last twenty-four hours? When was the last time you felt most grateful?

I haven't even attempted to answer all the questions she has asked me so far, but I will eventually. Right now, I have to get to bed as tomorrow I have to be at Bangkok train station at eight a.m. to board the Eastern Oriental Express. I would have loved to have stayed in Bangkok longer to explore the city, however tomorrow is the only date I can catch this train that fits into my travel schedule. Pity...

I will stay on this train for four days and four nights, stopping in Kuala Lumpur, Malaysia, for two days. On the train, they have sleeping carriages, and I can look at the menu online; the menu is first class with the highest quality wine. Once I get to Singapore, I will stay in the famous Raffles hotel for two nights. All-inclusive will cost three thousand dollars. Usually, one single night in the Raffles hotel would cost seven hundred dollars. I realise this part of my adventure is costly, but I'll never get another chance like this again. I want to savour every minute of it!

I arrived at Bangkok train station early to ensure I didn't miss the train. As I'm sitting here, two monks in orange robes walk by me; how surreal. It's eighty percent Buddhism in Thailand. Others that will be travelling on the Eastern Oriental Express are slowly arriving. Everyone is excited, and the sense of adventure is heightened. The local Thai people are selling snacks and souvenirs on the station platform. I bought a few souvenir trinkets with the little bit of Thai Baht currency I had. It's pretty humid, considering it is early morning.

All the passengers are boarding the train now, and I get shown to my sleeping carriage with all my belongings. The train's interior is of the highest quality, decorated to the time frame of the Nineteenth Century.

I've made my way to the lounge area of the train, which has a very cosy and relaxing ambience. The tone of the atmosphere is set, and everyone is in a good mood and ready to enjoy their excursion over the next few days. By their animated faces and enthusiastic conversations, you could almost smell people's expectations of how the trip would be.

As we pulled out of Bangkok station, I peered out the window and saw that we were leaving the big city, its concrete buildings, and the population of ten million. The total population in Thailand is seventy million – twice the population of Canada, although you could fit Thailand into one province in Canada quite easily. Then I could see small bamboo shacks appearing where families were living and doing their daily chores, washing their clothes, and cooking. I made my way to the dining carriage to have breakfast. The whole décor throughout the train is luxurious. As I was having breakfast, I stared out of the window at the scenery, and I just wanted to soak up the whole experience of the train ride through southeast Asia. They told us that we would stop at certain towns where we could disembark and look around the city if we so wished. The main stopover will be in Kula Lumpa in

Malaysia, and we will spend two nights in a five-star hotel and have a tour around the city. When we are off the train, the staff have time for the logistics of restocking food, bedding, etc. My little guidebook of Southeast Asia, which I purchased at Toronto's airport bookshop just before I boarded the plane for England, says Malaysia has a population of thirty-three million. The capital, Kuala Lumpur, has almost two million, and the currency there is the ringgit.

Sitting in the lounge section of the train, I mentioned to a couple of people I was talking to that I have a friend back in Canada who has written some questions for me to try and answer on my travels. They were intrigued and eager to know what they were, so I told them, and they all gave their opinion of what they considered the answers were. Most of them had different answers, so I suppose I could say the responses were subjective, but interesting, nonetheless. I retired to my sleeping carriage reasonably early; the months of travelling and jet lag took their toll.

The last two days on the train have been amazing. This morning, the Eastern Oriental Express arrived in Kuala Lumpur, the capital of Malaysia. The city is located in the west-central area of Peninsular Malaysia and about forty kilometres east of its ocean port, Port Kelang, on the Strait of Malacca. Kuala Lumpur's modern skyline is dominated by the four hundred and fifty one metre tall Petronas Twin Towers – a pair of glass and steel clad skyscrapers with Islamic motifs. Approximately sixty three percent of the population is Muslim. The towers also offer a public sky bridge and observation deck. There were coaches to collect us from the train station and take us to our five-star hotels; one was the Mandarin Oriental, and the other was the Shangri La.

The next day, I travelled around in a rickshaw for most of the morning's sightseeing. Then, after lunch, we had a bus tour which took us to various tourist sights. On the bus, I met someone who had been in Thailand and Malaysia thirty years ago, and he said how much it had changed. He told me we see some countries when we travel, and that's it. But when we return years later, it has all changed. Naively you expect it to be the same, but everything is constantly changing. Travelling down through Thailand and Malaysia, it was noticeable how poor the people were. When you see first-hand how so many people live in poverty, it humbles you and makes *you think how grateful you are to have clean running water and enough food to eat back in your country. Apparently, Singapore is in contrast to Thailand and Malaysia; Singapore is clean and modern, and the Singapore dollar is strong and economically doing fine, so I've been told. Chinese and English are spoken there, and everything is written in both languages. Singapore is a clean and law-abiding country. In a few days, I will see for myself if all that is accurate or not.*

When I eventually reach Singapore, I'm looking forward to visiting Tiffany's on Orchard Road and having afternoon tea at Raffles.

As I sat on a bench outside the front of my hotel, standing just a short distance from me were two monks who I overheard explaining something to a young German couple who are apparently touring south-east Asia. The monks told the couple that they are from the Dhamma Sakyamuni Monastery and reside in one of the last remaining limestone cave temples in Malaysia, which sits nestled into the foot of Mount Kanthan in the limestone hills that rise up from the Kinta Valley. The couple asked the monks if they could offer some wisdom on helping them navigate through their life in this materialistic world and what they would have to do to be happy. The monks were glad to oblige. They explained to the couple that all happiness dependent on others would disappear sooner or later. It is temporary, it is momentary, and it is illusory. Only that joy is ours, which wells up within your own being. Hence, Buddha says, "Delight in solitude." Aloneness is the joy of being just yourself. It is being joyous with yourself; it is enjoying your own company.

There are very few people who enjoy their own company, but they want or expect other people to enjoy their company. If they don't enjoy it, they feel insulted, alone, and disgusted with themselves. In fact, if you cannot enjoy your own company, who else will enjoy it? Aloneness and solitude are positive. It is overflowing joy for no reason. It is our very nature to be joyous; hence, there is no need to depend on anybody else. There is no other motive in it; it is simply there. Just as the water flows downwards, your being rises upwards. Just give it a chance; give it solitude. Compose yourself, and be happy. You are a seeker.

They went on to explain principles.

The Principle of Mentalism – everything is the mind,

and the universe is mental. Thoughts lead to the manifestation of things and events, and thoughts create our state of existence and the quality of our experience here on earth. Therefore, be responsible for everything you create by being responsible for everything that you think.

The Principle of Vibration – nothing rests, everything moves, everything vibrates. At the most fundamental level, the universe and everything comprising it is pure vibrational energy manifesting itself in solidity. Matter is merely energy in a state of vibration.

The Principle of Polarity – everything is dual. Everything has poles, and everything has its opposite. Opposites are identical in nature but different in degree. Extremes meet, and all paradoxes may be reconciled.

The Principle of Rhythm – everything flows out and in. Everything has its tides, and all things rise and fall. The pendulum-swing manifests in everything. The swing to the right is the measure of the swing to the left. Rhythm compensates.

The Principle of Cause and Effect – every cause has its effect, and every effect has its cause. Everything happens according to law, and chance is but a name for *law not recognised. There are many planes of causation, but nothing escapes the law.*

Principle of Gender – gender is in everything. Everything has its masculine and feminine principles. Gender manifests on all planes.

They carried on to explain synchronicity.

Synchronicity has a numinous quality, and numinosity provokes a deep sense of wonder and mystery. It is a term derived from the Latin numen, meaning 'arousing spiritual or religious emotion; mysterious or awe-inspiring'. Synchronicity is seemingly unrelated events that are not connected by Cause and Effect but are connected by meaning. They clarified Spiritual Currencies – this analogy can be seen readily in the sayings 'Spending Time' and 'Paying Attention'. Whatever information or endeavours we put our time and attention toward, we end up getting something in return for that investment. So, we must be aware of what we spend our time on. What we are spending our time doing. Also, what we are paying attention to.

Karma – Karma is a word meaning the result of a person's actions as well as the actions themselves. It is a term about the cycle of Cause and Effect. According to the theory of Karma, what happens to a person happens because they caused it with their actions. The first thing you must do before anything is to understand yourself first. What are your core values and morals? Live by them if you want to align with the life you want to live. When you avoid pain, you're avoiding meaning; we need to sacrifice for purpose and meaning. They informed the couple that if they wanted to lead a content and satisfying life, they should not have a bucket list, but a detachment list. To try and live as a minimalist. Wanting less is better. Not having more is good. Buy only what you need, not what you want. Have fewer expectations about anything, then you won't be disappointed so much. The young couple thanked the monks, and everyone departed.

I had to try and digest everything that had happened for a few minutes. Me sitting on a bench in Kuala Lumpur, listening to monks explain to a German couple about karma, vibration and synchronicity; how bizarre is that! If someone back in Canada seven or eight months ago had told me that would happen to me, I would have thought they were crazy. I have to admit, many bizarre things have happened to me on this trip. So many experiences I will never forget.

All of that was so fascinating. I will have to reread that later to ensure I understand it completely. One thing I wish they had explained is about death. What happens when we die? The day I was on my way here to this cabin, I wondered: who will remember me when I die? I haven't done anything extraordinary. I'm not famous, and nobody will even miss me. Would anyone remember me besides my parents? When I think of my parents' situation, I think their loyalty and integrity to each other stopped them from moving on. They sacrificed their dreams and freedom, their potential destiny, for their significant other. Perhaps they gave up what they really wanted to do so they could take care of me.

Kuala Lumpa is the halfway marker between Thailand and Singapore on this train journey. I watched the remaining passengers returning to the railway station to board the Eastern Oriental Express so we could continue our trip southward to Singapore. While seated in the lounge area of the train, I struck up a conversation with a middle-aged man and told him of the encounter I had overhearing the two monks and the young German couple. He told me he was a mathematician and asked if I was interested in Pythagoras and his explanation. Of course, I was curious and immediately said yes. He told me our stories have tremendous power, and one story that we are often told is that our lives are completely random. Life can't be understood logically, and as our world becomes ever so advanced, the more unpredictable things seem, and the more anxious and frustrated we become. But what if we could tell a different story that tells us that our world is actually made up of patterns on top of patterns? That history only repeats itself, that there is an astonishing level of order in the universe and, if you watch closely, what we call chaos is just patterns we hadn't yet noticed. And underlying all of it is a level of organization in symmetry that holds it all together.

The idea that the universe follows predictable patterns is actually ancient. One of the earlier sources comes from an ancient Greek philosopher-mathematician named Pythagoras, who lived in approximately 570 BC. Pythagoras was a vegetarian and believed in gender equality. He was interested in science and mathematics; this would form the basis for what many consider to be his most important work – numerology. It's one of the oldest systems of knowledge, and precisely these insights would lead Pythagoras to believe that numbers had a divine essence and that connecting with numbers was to communicate with the divine. To understand numerology, we have to look at four essential ideas. The first is that the universe is mathematical. Pythagoras believed that numbers are the most essential elements in nature, and understanding them is the gateway to unlocking all of reality. According to Pythagoras, there are two basic levels to our universe; the first level is the physical world, which is the world we can see and touch and experience with our senses. But one level below this is an abstract and mathematical structure which underlies our entire universe. A world of numbers and geometry. Reality is a fine-tuned universe.

The second concept in numerology is the idea that our universe moves through cycles. When we look at nature, we see constant birth and rebirth, the cycles of day and night, the seasons in the year, and even the cycles of life and death. This is something that has long been understood in Chinese Numerology as well. We see this in an idea called Wu Xing, also known as the Five Elements of Nature. These elements were believed to move in a continuous cycle repeated endlessly, giving rise to everything we see all around us. Our own modern *science has uncovered all sorts of cycles in nature, including the lunar cycles of the moon, planetary cycles, and the nitrogen cycle. Our world follows a basic rhythm with a pattern that replays itself repeatedly. But it's not just nature; it also applies to us. According to numerology, our lives follow an Epicycle that lasts nine years. Each year of your life has its unique vibration, energy, and approach that leads to growth and happiness. And it's only when you work with the energy of your cycle that you can take advantage of the opportunities around you. But when you work against that energy, you struggle to move ahead. What makes this even more challenging is that we live in a world obsessed with early achievement, and we often put enormous pressure on ourselves to find success. If it doesn't happen as quickly as we would like, we become anxious and frustrated. But notice how nature doesn't force itself to meet deadlines. Nature unfolds on its own, in its own time, the way it's supposed to. It takes uncommon wisdom and patience to wait for things to reveal themselves without forcing them when the timing isn't right. So, what does this mean for you? It means that your numbers reveal a divine timing in your life, a time for education, a* career, a time for relationships, or a time for a family. And because life presents so many important choices, it's essential to understand your nine-year cycle. The third idea is a discovery that music and numbers are intimately connected. Pythagoras found that different notes in music have a mathematical relationship with each other. In fact, the language of music is the language of fractions and ratios. He found that three mathematical relationships were especially beautiful to listen to; he called them octaves, fifths, and fourths. Of course, these are all numbers. These insights lead Pythagoras to the idea that the universe itself also vibrates to its own music in the same way that every string in a harp vibrates at its own pitch, as does every planet in space. Pythagoras believed that as the celestial bodies move through space, they create beautiful music, but not in the usual sense because human ears cannot hear it. He called this idea 'Musica Universalis', commonly known as the 'Music of the Spheres'. Pythagoras believed this was the highest form of music in that it followed a perfect mathematical harmony in precision.

Interestingly, this idea isn't as far-fetched as you might think. This suggests that there is a fundamental underlying mathematical organisation in the universe. But it's not just planets in space; according to numerology, you have a unique vibration, too, and so does every human being and creature on earth. If you really think about it, we often think about being in tune with people we get along with or being on the same wavelength, and we also talk about specific people resonating with us. But isn't it interesting that tuning, wavelength, and resonance are all ideas relating to vibration? The idea that everything in the universe has its own vibration also finds support in a scientific concept known as string theory. When we look at nature through the lens of string theory, we find that the universe is a grand cosmic symphony. String theory was discovered in 1968, and numerology described the universe in terms of vibration more than two thousand years ago.

The fourth idea in numerology is known as metempsychosis, or the transmigration of souls. Pythagoras believed that the soul is immortal, that it is the part of us that makes us who we are, and which survives after we die. Essentially, the soul is trapped in a cycle of death and rebirth. The only way to break free from this cycle is to understand the lessons we have been *brought here to learn. If we don't learn those lessons, we are doomed to repeat the same problems repeatedly until we do. A lot of the pain and suffering we experience in our lives is a direct result of ignoring our life lessons. The idea of the soul is compelling and shows up in almost every culture worldwide. But is there any evidence to suggest that souls exist? To understand the soul, we must look at death's meaning. Historically, doctors define death as the moment when we stop breathing and the heart stops beating. But, people who have had near-death experiences (NDEs) and have returned from the brink of death describe very similar things. They talk about feeling a profound sense of peace, seeing a bright warm light, and believing that their soul carries on beyond their physical body when they die.*

Pythagoras' most significant legacy is the idea that numbers can reveal the patterns and cycles of our lives. At the heart of numerology is the idea that each of us is born at a particular time and place, which makes us totally unique in the universe. Each of us is a combination of experiences with individual strengths and talents, and every single one of us is formed in a way that has never happened before and will never happen again.

So, understand your numbers, because, as we will see, that's the key to unlocking who you are, why you're here, and the adaptabilities that already exist within you.

According to the theory of Nikola Tesla's 'three, six, nine', one to nine digital root numbers exist. All other higher or lower numbers are a combination of those digital root numbers. Nikola Tesla's 'three, six, nine' theory is alleged to 'hold the key to the universe'. Threes appeared often in human history, and triangles have three sides – as do pyramids. Trinities are abound in human history, as in the Father, Son, and Holy Ghost. Tesla would point to the trifecta of energy, frequency, and vibration, which he believed contained the secrets of the universe.

In numerology, it is believed that every person goes through a nine-year cycle continuously. As one nine-year cycle is completed, a new one begins.

The nine-year Cycle is: year one – beginning; year two – connecting; year three – creating; year four – building; year five – changing; year six – nurturing; year seven – re-valuating; year eight – expanding; year nine – completing.

The stages of the cycle are:

One – Beginning.

In year one, you need to re-examine your goals. This is the year that lays down the foundation for all the years in the new cycle. This would be an excellent year to start new projects. Your primary focus should be on yourself and your life's passions and goals.

Two – Connecting.

Year two will be a year you need to focus on your relationship with others. Now is important to listen and compromise, and you need to be sensitive to the needs of others. This will be a slow but valuable year.

Three – Creating.

Year three will be a year you need to express yourself, to come in touch with your true feelings and emotions. This may be done in so many different ways; through socialising, writing, singing, painting, dancing, and so on. This is about telling the truth as you see it. This year can be both agonising and inspirational.

Four – Building.

In year four, it may be that you will have a lot of hard work to do. This is when you should lay down a solid foundation for your future and get things in order. On the practical side, it may propose taking care of business, such as securing your home or starting a family. On the emotional level, it may be to finally begin the task of digging into your roots. If you have unsolved issues in your past, this is the year to straighten things out.

Five – Changing.

Year five is all about change in almost any aspect. It could involve getting a new job or moving to a new location. Perhaps you discover a new skill you want to master. Needless to say, this is an excellent year to travel and expand your horizons. On a deeper level, it could involve a change in inner beliefs.

Six – Nurturing.

Year six is all about your loved ones. During this year, it will be imperative to care for and show your family members appreciation. This is a time when your life revolves around your family.

Seven – Re-evaluating.

Year seven is about ensuring you get time to meditate in solitude. Re-examine your core values. You may want to seek advice from a healer or someone you trust. If you ever dreamed of taking a Sabbath year, this would be a great time to do that. This is a year for cleansing. It is also a year of legal matters. There is a high probability that legal disputes will be resolved during the year.

Eight – Expanding.

In year eight, you are meant to empower yourself. This is when you need to step up and lead; be the boss. Take responsibility and be the authority. Show that you are capable of being in charge. It could be something in your daily life, such as taking charge of organising a school event. It could also be stepping up as a leading power figure in a company. This is about power. Don't abuse power. Remember, with power also comes responsibility and integrity.

Nine – Completing.

This is the final year of the nine-year cycle. Completion and closure are keywords this year; this is the time to come to terms with all you have accomplished during the current cycle.

I find all this information fascinating, and it came from people I would not expect it to come from. When I interact with people, they seem like a puzzle. Life is a puzzle, an enigma waiting to be solved. If we could regress back to how we were when we were children – the way we thought, childlike, simpler, not so complicated – we would be more content and satisfied.

We could cut out all the false beliefs, and our minds wouldn't be so cluttered. We could think more clearly without distractions and bias influencing everyone. Perhaps we would see the world as it truly is. If we could peel back all the layers of unnecessary judgements and assumptions, we would see things more clearly, without the façade. I suppose, in short – don't make things complicated. Keep things simple. The less clutter, the better – in the physical and our minds.

Chapter Nine

Thailand – Malaysia – Singapore – part two

'Travel enables the spirit and does away with our prejudices.'

- Oscar Wilde -

May-June

This train journey from Thailand, through Malaysia, to Singapore has a unique sense of adventure on the Eastern Oriental Express. We are experiencing a glamorous, outlandish, colourful life. Compared to when we stop at numerous villages and cities, it is interestingly strange and unusual from what the passengers are accustomed to in their countries.

As I was seated at my table for the evening meal, I glanced out the window and noticed it was slowly getting dark outside, and I could see the sun setting in the distance. I could faintly hear the wheels of the train gliding over the railway tracks. Other passengers entered the dining carriage; everyone's attire was suitable for the evening meal to make it that little bit more special. In the background, I heard a gentleman order a gin and tonic, and while I slowly drank my red wine, I opened the next brown envelope with the seven questions. They were as follows:

When was the last time you had a deep connection to someone? When was the last time you laughed so hard? What makes you lose sleep? What was your last good deed for someone you didn't know? If you die suddenly, what would your family find in your belongings? Does your life have meaning? What is humanity's biggest potential waste?

I laid the list on top of the envelope on the table and contemplated what she must be going through at this moment. But I promised myself before I left Canada that I would concentrate on myself for this trip and not think or worry about other people. It isn't easy, though. I wonder if she is in pain. We are all experiencing some sort of pain in one way or another. Either physical or mental.

Everyone experiences pain, and most suffer from patterns that continue to make life miserable unless something or someone intervenes. The pain we feel comes from the energies that keep curving back and cancelling *the wise self and the good word that waits to be expressed from within us. Persistent pain usually indicates that we have been trapped in a life too small for our true nature. That is the usual human fate and the common predicament where the little self obscures the greater nature behind it. Until people realise what harms them and limits them from within, they are unlikely to call out for someone to help stop the pain. The remedy may be nearby, but until the pain becomes unbearable, most remain caught in the agony of one form or another of self-inflicted wounds. As Rumi said, 'The cure for pain is in the pain.'*

Some people could hear you speak a thousand words and still not understand you. And others will understand without you even saying a word.

One of the biggest mistakes we make is assuming that other people think the way we think. If there's one bit of advice I would give to my daughter, it would be: it's never too late to be whoever you want to be. I hope you live a life you're proud of, and if you find that you're not, I hope you have the strength to start over.

As I've travelled, I have been mindful of what I eat daily, trying to live a healthy lifestyle as much as I possibly can. At different stages of my journey, I have undergone fasting for short periods.

I had an inner dialogue with myself last night regarding all the wisdom I have attained on this journey; my higher self explained it to me. I've noticed, over the years, that people tend to create negative stories and self-images about themselves. Therefore, they are convinced they can't get what they want. But what seems impossible for you might be closer or easier than you think. I wonder how many times people give up just before a breakthrough. Every problem comes with a solution; never trick yourself into thinking you did everything possible. The right skills and knowledge are between you and what you want. Everything in your life is a reflection of the choices you have made. If you want different results, make other choices. Remember, we are spiritual beings playing characters. Meaning we are not the characters. We are actors.

There is nothing good or bad in this world. It is our mind that labels things as good or bad. So, there is nothing really wrong with the current version of you. It is your mind's dissatisfaction with it that creates misery. Your choices create a new reality for you every single *day. Just make a choice to change – to be another version of yourself. Life is inherently neutral – you attach positive and negative meanings to events, thus charging the events with emotions to go either in a negative or positive timeline. Accept a negative situation, and don't give it any more attention. Starve it for attention, and it will not disturb you anymore. Forget about it; otherwise, you give it importance. As Carl Jung would say: 'Until you make the unconscious conscious, it will direct your life, and you will call it fate.'*

Many of us have to make decisions that define who we are and what we believe in. Most often, the choices we face may seem insignificant, but this doesn't mean that they're not important to us. Even the smallest action can impact our self-respect, integrity, and, ultimately, our reputation.

There are several reasons why integrity is so important. First, living a life of integrity means never having to spend time or energy questioning ourselves. Life becomes simple when we listen to our hearts and do the right thing. Our life and actions are open for everyone to see, and we don't have to worry about hiding anything.

Integrity defines your values, and you can't live by values if you don't know what you truly believe in. So, start by defining your core values which you will not compromise on, no matter the consequence.

Analyse every choice you make. Often, people cut corners or make bad choices when they think no one is watching. Having integrity means that, no matter what, you make the right choice – especially when no one is watching. You'll usually know what's right and wrong, although sometimes you might need some quiet time to figure it out. If you're unsure what the right choice is, ask yourself this question: if I make this choice, will I feel okay with myself afterwards? Honesty and integrity aren't values you should live by only when it's convenient; they're values you should live by always. This includes the big and little choices that no one sees.

I remember my mother used to encourage integrity. She used to say people with integrity often have the same characteristics. They are humble, have a strong sense of self, have high self-esteem, and are self-confident. These characteristics are important because you'll sometimes be under intense pressure from others to make the wrong choice. You must value your own time, so you can also value other people's time. Give credit where it is due, don't take credit for things you didn't do. You must always credit those who deserve it. My mother was authentic. You wouldn't catch her in a lie or being fake. She was always honest. She was honest and didn't feel the need to lie as it was important for her to get to where she needed to get in life honestly. She would never take advantage of others. She was not a person who would take advantage of someone else. She loved to build people up and help them get where they needed to be. Taking too much from someone else will never be an issue with someone with a lot of integrity. She did not argue over disagreements. She would talk through things in a civil manner or not talk at all. You could not force this person into arguing over something completely ridiculous.

I find this to be a very respectable trait. She gave most people the benefit of the doubt. She tried to see the good in everyone. I think this is because she felt like maybe more people in this world also have integrity. That being said, if you took advantage of her too much, she would get rid of you. She knew when something was bothering someone. She had a great intuition that let her know when something was going on. If someone was down in the dumps, she would notice. Chances are she would actually do what she could to cheer you up. She believed others. She accepted your word as truth until it was disproven, but she didn't take lying well, and once you lied to her, it was unlikely that she would ever take your word again. She apologised first. She would come to you and apologise if she had done something wrong. This is just how she was. She would own up to her mistake and try to make things right. She was humble. She didn't quite know her own worth. She did so much good she didn't quite see it. In her life, she was always helping other people. She loved to know she had improved someone's life; it gave her life meaning. She was always kind to those who needed it. Giving kindness can go a long way. Mom, you were someone with true integrity; thank you for being who you were and for all you did. You made a difference in society. If you felt no one else was proud of you, know that I am. You made me the person I am. I never realised how much you influenced me until today. Thank you, Mom, so much! I love you!

The Eastern Oriental Express' last stop is in Johor Bahru, the capital of the Malaysian state of Johor, which sits at the southern tip of the Malay Peninsula. We will spend the last two nights in Malaysia in the Hilton Hotel before carrying on with our journey by coach via a causeway across the straits of Johor, connecting it to Singapore. This wasn't planned as the last stop, but urgent repairs to the track needed attention, which nobody foresaw. After getting checked into my room at the Hilton, I wanted to find a drug store to buy some vitamin pills and perhaps some tonic for keeping my immune system up, as I sometimes feel a bit run down from travelling. While in the pharmacy, I noticed some cards on the counter advertising that a hospital in Singapore was searching for volunteer participants, specifically westerners, to participate in a medical study dealing with psychedelics. I was curious about this, and I asked the woman behind the counter about the study.

She explained that psychedelics, also known as hallucinogens, are a class of psychoactive substances that produce changes in perception, mood, and cognitive processes. Psychedelics affect all the senses, altering a person's thinking, sense of time, and emotions. Apparently, the hospital will use some sort of Psilocybin-based medicine found in truffles and mushrooms.

Psilocybin, the active ingredient in the hallucinogenic fungus, resets the parts of the brain involved in depression and anxiety. They have also found that seventy five percent of the patients with alcohol and nicotine addictions have stopped after taking micro-doses of the treatment with this Psilocybin-based medicine. She went on to inform me that the hospital found all the benefits she mentioned to me in the first part of the empirical study, and in the second part of the study, they wanted to find out how long the benefits last. As a nurse, this was fascinating to me. If this worked with no side effects, this could be very useful for people in Canada struggling with depression, anxiety, and alcohol and nicotine addictions.

Our last two nights in Malaysia have ended, and we are on the coaches that will take us on the causeway to Singapore.

We arrived at Raffles, where we will spend the next two nights, and I must say it looks majestic! As we stood in the foyer, ready to check in, I glanced around; it's stunning.

I saw a hotel guest protesting to one of the staff members about something I felt was trivial. The hotel staff member attempted to persuade the guest to move to the side so she wouldn't disturb the other guests, who could hear and see what was happening, but she was adamant about not complying with the hotel staff member. She continued complaining about something petty. As I witnessed this, I remembered what a fellow nurse once said.

How people treat you is simply a direct reflection of how they feel about themselves. Do not take it personally. People will act consistently with how they view themselves to be, whether the view is accurate or not. People tend to project what they feel inside, or lack within themselves, onto others. Again, do not take it personally. Haters don't really hate you. They hate themselves. When you put people's opinions of you onto a pedestal, you open yourself up to doubts and fears. We are all created equally, and we all have value to share. Never treat yourself less than others, and never put anyone on a pedestal. Never be intimidated by looks or status; never let fear hijack you emotionally and prevent you from getting what you deserve. One day you will realise people's opinions of you are not your reality or problem.

I finally got shown to my room. I've gotten to the stage now, after staying in so many hotels and people's houses, that I go into autopilot in unpacking my belongings to prioritise what I need first. Then, I orientate myself in my new surroundings and explore the immediate vicinity outside. Then I purchase the local newspaper to read what's happening in the local area. All of this has become a habit now. I can see why people get addicted to travelling. It is a constant stimulus for your mind and a relentless stream of information that you are absorbing continuously: the ongoing learning of different currencies in each country, their unique customs and religions, ensuring you don't offend them by what you say or do, etc.

Travelling is definitely for you if you are curious by nature. From my travels so far, I have become aware that most of us, if not all, are searching for something in our lives. It starts with finding the right partner, a job, the dream house, etc. Then, eventually, when you think you have everything you wanted, you still feel a void, that something is still missing, but you don't know what. Some people think it's material items, so they buy copious amounts of stuff, but that's not it. Over the years, we have been covered by layers of opinions and beliefs from people telling us what we should and shouldn't do, which has buried our true authentic selves. We think we should be doing and saying things to people so they will like us instead of listening to our heart and what our soul desires. We wouldn't need other people to validate us if we did this. We have to strip back layer by layer until we find ourselves again. The elusive thing people feel is missing and have the unconscious urge to find is their 'true self'. Whilst travelling, I've been waiting for this epiphany to happen. But I've realised it's not sudden; it's gradual. In each person I have met and spoken to, I have detected a bit of me in them – positive and negative. They have all taught me something about myself. It's as though they were all there at that precise time and place to help me, and vice versa.

As I sit in the park just off Orchard Road, I read a pamphlet I took from the hotel lobby that explains a few facts and figures about Singapore, and highlights tourist attractions and places of interest. Singapore was founded as a British trading colony in 1819 and, in 1965, became independent. At present, there are 5.6 million people residing in Singapore. It mentions a visit to Little China and Little India on Dunlop Street. Another place they encourage you to visit is the Infinity Pool on the fifty seventh floor of the Marina Bay Sands Hotel; the view from there is supposed to be spectacular. While walking down Orchard Road earlier, I went into one of the shopping malls to get something to eat at one of the food courts, which, I must say, has numerous kinds of cuisine. As I sit here in the park, my mind starts to wander; I start reminiscing about the time I was in the UAE with the students, and I asked one of them about 'woke people' and what 'woke' actually meant. A young lady explained that woke means alert to injustice in society, especially racism. "We need to stay angry and stay woke," she had said. The word 'woke' – to stay 'woke' – is not new, it began appearing in the 1940s. African Americans first used it to literally mean becoming woken up or sensitised to issues of justice.

Why I thought of that, I don't know. Maybe I'm just trying to make sense of everything that has happened to me since I left Canada. The hardships some people have to endure during their lives because of war and poverty, and the life I have had up until now is no comparison. I have always had enough food and a place to live, and *have been relatively healthy my whole life. I have never had to suffer like many people around the world. You would think I would be more grateful because of this. But I still have trouble sleeping some nights, and I wake up, scared, like I'm falling.*

I still have this relentless need to discover who I genuinely am and what the primary purpose I'm here to accomplish is.

My opinion is that there is a talent we have that is buried inside of us, laying dormant, that has to be excavated, which I feel is what we should be doing to reveal who or what we are or can be. I think many people underestimate themselves and what they are capable of achieving.

I remember one of the girls in the UAE said, "You either get busy living or keep on dying." She said we should have a dream, a mental destination. A dream can be fuel to drive the supposedly impossible to reality. We should allow ourselves to frequent small treats to prove we are worthy. She also said we should give ourselves a project to express our inner life and what we are passionate about, and find at least one good friend who gets you that you can talk about anything and everything with. The short period I spent with those students made me feel young again; they seemed to know they were on the cusp of endless opportunities. It was just a question of what one they would choose. Their attitude was carefree and optimistic. It was a joy to be around them. So, I will carry on exploring a little bit more of Singapore.

The authenticity was uncanny when I walked around Little China and Little India; it was just like being back in actual China and India. Eventually, I got a taxi back to my hotel in time for afternoon tea. The cakes and scones were delicious. An Egyptian businessman at my table spoke about the mysterious Egyptian pyramids. It was an interesting conversation, to say the least. He told me that the Giza pyramid is four hundred and eighty one feet high, weighs six million tons, and was built from 2.5 million stone blocks. The footprint this covers is thirteen acres. There are all kinds of theories on who built the great pyramids and how; all very fascinating.

Chapter Ten

Kenya

'Life is either a daring adventure or nothing.'

- Helen Keller -

July

I arrived at Nairobi Jomo Kenyatta International Airport, and the hotel sent a Range Rover to pick me up. I went through the usual procedure of sorting myself out when I got to my hotel. Kenya was another country I was looking forward to; just like the Middle East, the adventurous side of it intrigued me. I booked a safari through the hotel I was staying at, which will take me through the Maasai Mara for over three weeks. There would be overnight stays in lodges next to water holes where we would be able to observe the animals gathering to drink. Maasai tribe members would be our security throughout the safari. The Maasai are well known for the heights they can jump to.

The safari started from Nairobi and returned to Nairobi after three weeks. I travelled in a minibus where the sunroof could be taken out, and I could stand up and peer out over the vast wilderness. I shared the minibus with a few of other people. The people on the safari were allocated into small groups. In my group was a father from Austria who had recently become a widower; he was with his teenage daughter. After his wife died, he promised his daughter they would go on a safari together in Africa, and now he is fulfilling that promise. He was trying to numb his daughter's pain from losing her mother. He was trying to dampen his sadness, too. I could notice he was trying to stay strong for his daughter. A British couple who had just married was also part of my group. We all seemed compatible with one another and got along fine. James was our driver – a fitting name, I thought. James taught me some words in Swahili. He also explained a little about wildlife and the cost of essential items in Kenyan Shillings. It was very informative.

After breakfast, we didn't eat anything until the evening meal. Throughout the day, we drank isotonic fluids to keep hydrated due to our electrolytes being lost through sweating in the hot weather. However, in the early evening, when we reached the next lodge we would be staying at overnight, a magnificent feast of food was laid out for us. With our appetites, it didn't take much encouragement to get us to start eating.

The lodges were built on stilts high off the ground, and at dusk we could look down at the water holes where the animals were drinking; it was an incredible sight to witness. From the day's heat, the evening, with its cool breeze, was welcomed by all of us. We could hear the wildlife out in the bush where it was pitch black. There were verandas on the other side of the lodges where we could sit outside, enjoy a beverage of our choosing, and converse about what we had experienced that day. We had the Maasai tribe patrolling around our lodge every night to ensure no animals would creep onto the level where we were residing.

One day we were approaching a lake and saw a blanket of pink along the shore for miles and miles. As we got closer, we noticed thousands upon thousands of flamingos. So extraordinary! As we drove around the lake, we drove alongside herds of hundreds of wilder-beasts and zebras; it was breath-taking to see the number of them galloping along, and the noise was incredible! We also took a one-day hot air balloon flight over

Maasai Mara National Reserve. On this hot sunny day, we silently drifted over different species of wildlife in their natural habitat; it was epic! Because the flight was silent, it didn't disturb the animals too much; only the sight of the balloon made them apprehensive. The flight was so therapeutic, calm, and relaxing. The birds-eye view was like having a sense of freedom. There was no noise, only the sounds of nature, animals, and the occasional noise of flames from the bursts of gas allotted by the pilot to keep us airborne. I've taken many photos throughout my travels, but these particular ones from the hot air balloon flight are special.

When we eventually returned to Nairobi, we visited the renowned Nairobi market. Then, a few of us obtained transport to take us to Mombasa. I acquired short-term accommodation in a thatched hut with bamboo furniture directly on what was called Shelly Beach. Two days later, I moved into a small hotel approximately five hundred metres from the beach. Once I had moved into the hotel, I met a small guy called Reseaky, who was responsible for cleaning my room. He was polite and pleasant to speak to. He mentioned one day he would be taking his girlfriend to the cinema that evening and then for a meal.

He asked me if I would like to join them. I think he felt sorry for me being alone all the time. I agreed, on the condition he allowed me to pay for everything that evening. He said it would be okay, but he would feel awkward if people saw me paying. So, we agreed that I would give him the money before we went out, and he would pay the appropriate people.

Reseaky, his girlfriend and I caught the bus a short distance from the hotel to take us to Mombasa to the cinema. It was strange being on the bus only with black people, me being the only white person. I realised this is how they must feel in Canada or Europe. As we entered the cinema, I could see the movie had already started; we'd arrived ten minutes late because I was not ready at the hotel. As our eyes finally adjusted to the darkness, we eventually found our seats. Above us, attached to the ceiling, were what I can only describe as propellers from old planes, swirling around in a clockwise motion, acting as the air-conditioning. I noticed once the movie finished that I was the only westerner; it felt strange, but everyone smiled and was friendly to me. Since I have been in Kenya, everyone has been welcoming, kind, and pleasant to me. After watching the movie, we went for a lovely *meal. When we had finished the meal, I decided to open the next brown envelope. I asked Reseaky and his girlfriend if they wouldn't mind listening to the questions and if they could give me their opinion. With big smiles, they enthusiastically agreed.*

The seven questions in the envelope were:

When you're old and grey, what would you consider the most outstanding achievement of your life? Do you truly know yourself? Are you doing things only because society tells you that you should? Or are you doing things because they genuinely make you happy? What is the meaning of success to you? Do you consider your life's work worthy enough? When do you feel truly alive?

Their opinions on the questions were interesting, coming from Kenyans, but not the same as I would have expected from Canadians, which I thought was quite unique, having the chance to hear perspectives from another nationality. I told them I had watched very little TV since leaving Canada, especially the news. I've gone onto social media a couple of times, but they can sometimes distort the truth; fake news always seems to be floating around. They asked me about my travels. I told them it's all well and good seeing all the beautiful sights in all the countries; however, if you can't experience it with someone you are very close with or love, it doesn't seem to have the same value.

Jane is good at shifting focus amongst different tasks and contexts. Jane talks about fake news. I've had my share of fake news and fake people. Especially last week when I found some photos of my parents from before I came on the scene; those photos define them as entirely different from how they are now – their demeanour is so different. In the earlier pictures, they were smiling and having fun and dressed fashionably; they seemed natural and genuine.

Then I discovered the adoption papers and read that my parents are not my biological parents. That was devastating. My whole life was a lie, and I felt betrayed by them and unworthy that they hadn't told me. Besides, why did my birth parents give me up? I feel abandoned by them, unwanted and unloved. This was the last reason from many that made me decide to come to the cabin to end my life. If it wasn't for Jane and her journal giving me that tiny spark of hope, I wouldn't still be here. I had given up on myself and felt that I was not even worth being here for anyone, let alone me.

They say that the human race is doomed: we have lost touch with nature, the media has corrupted us, and the planet has no future. I can't entirely agree; I believe that humanity is full of hope and that our salvation lies within each of us. I know what is coming towards my husband and I when we retire because I've already seen this with my husband when he was unemployed. Preparing for retirement is not just the financial side, but also the psychological side. When you retire or lose your job, you lose these five things:

One; structure. Two; identity. Three; relationships with work colleagues, some that had eventually become friends. Four; a sense of purpose. Five; a sense of power.

Reseaky and his girlfriend got a friend who drives taxis to take me back to the hotel while they got a bus back to their apartment. It was a pleasant evening, and we all enjoyed each other's company.

Walking along Shelly Beach this morning, there's not a single person in sight. Looking at the sky, I only see blue as far as I can look, not one single cloud to be seen. As I walk and feel the sun's warmth on my skin, I feel so relaxed and content. No worries, no anxiety about anything; I haven't felt like this for many years. I see some palm trees, so I walk over to them to sit in the shade for a while. I contemplate all the places I've been, the people I've met, and the experiences I've had over the months since I left Canada. Have I come any closer to discovering who I am, my authentic self, the genuine me? Yes and no; I've discovered more about my personality and know more about what I don't want in life, but I still haven't excavated the real me yet and what I sincerely want or desire. I honestly thought I would have learned who I was and what I wanted by now. I'm on the last stretch of my journey, homeward bound; in a couple of months, I'll be back in Canada. If I haven't gotten this figured out by then, has all this time, money, and effort been a waste? I know from this journey that I've changed; I see things differently, and feel I've become different. I hope my husband and daughter accept the person I've become. I can't imagine not having my husband and daughter in my life; that would be my ultimate loss. When I think about it, so many people are stuck on the treadmill in the rat race of life. They are not taking the time to take a step back and look at their overall situation. I have been fortunate to be able to do this, and I am so happy that I decided to do it. Otherwise, so many things go unnoticed and don't have the chance to get corrected. In this hurried, sped-up world we live in nowadays, we definitely have to take time out occasionally, otherwise, we will burn out.

Stop and smell the coffee, some people say. Well, I'm taking the time to smell the coffee; I hope it pays off. It's been a paradox; I've loved travelling, however, I'm not with my husband, and I miss my daughter. I wish we could have had all the experiences of my travels together. It's become apparent to me that as soon as I have some downtime to relax from the flights, train rides, etc., that I automatically think of my family, friends, and Canada. Then I start getting sentimental, nostalgic, melancholy, and homesick. I have to quickly snap myself out of it. I wonder if they have changed since I have been away. In my quiet times, when I can be alone, I tend to ponder over many things from my past, which is sometimes not good because I seem to overanalyse situations that happened, and you can't change the past, so I try not to dwell on that for too long or too often. When I look back, though, I wonder where all the years went; they have gone by so fast. One thing I have learned over the last months is to cherish 'the now' and be totally conscious of *the enjoyable things I am taking part in. I'm sure people underestimate how much time they have on this planet. You truly only appreciate it when you are in your later years. As a nurse, I have often treated people who have been drinking too much alcohol, smoking, and overeating at a relatively young age. Many of them are paying the price for it. Such a pity. It appears that most of the generation from fifteen to thirty-five years old are addicted to social media more than the rest of us.*

There was a time I was definitely addicted to it. I didn't respect, love, or value myself at that time. That's why last week I deleted all my social media accounts. I had had enough of everything; it was all too overwhelming. I used to try and show my parents my love for them by inserting a heart or an 'X' for a kiss after a text, or by sending, "I love you," but I'd get no response. I always felt they didn't care about me; I felt unloved. Most of the kids posted a grandiose life they were supposedly living, which was false. Most of them were envious of the others and posted nasty comments. Sometimes I wish I could return to times that I can remember as a small kid that were pleasant and happy.

A group of us went out on a small boat with a

transparent floor, and we could observe varieties of coloured fish swimming through the magnificent coral reef. I tried snorkelling and windsurfing as well. I traded some of my old clothes and an old watch for some wood carvings that some locals were carving on the beach.

I took a book from one of the lodges where I had stayed, which a fellow traveller had left behind. Two extracts from this book were:

'We rarely offer ourselves the time and space to consider; am I doing what I most want to do with my life? Do I ever know what that is? The noise in our heads and all around us drown out the 'still, small voice' inside. We are so busy doing 'something' that we rarely take a moment to look deeply and check in with our deepest desires.' Thich Nhat Hahn.

'What is poison? Anything which is more than our necessity is poison. It may be power, wealth, hunger, ego, greed, laziness, love, ambition, hate, or anything else. What is fear? Non-acceptance of uncertainty. If we accept that uncertainty, it becomes an adventure. What is envy? Non-acceptance of good in others; if we accept that good, it becomes inspirational. What is anger? Non-acceptance of things which are beyond our control. If we *accept, it becomes tolerance. What is hatred? Non-acceptance of a person as they are. If we accept a person unconditionally, it becomes love.' Rumi.*

I get the impression that we are all chasing something our whole lives. We spend time compulsively seeking something, but we're not exactly sure what. If we strip it all the way down, it's ultimately 'love'.

I want to write a letter and mail it at the post office, 'old school', as they used to do before e-mail or texting. I've never done that before; it would be my first time. How strange will that be? The letter would be to my adoptive parents explaining that I know they are not my birth parents, asking why they never told me, and, furthermore, asking them who my birth parents are. I missed genuine affection from my parents growing up, and I realise why now, because I wasn't their biological child. Perhaps that's why I got emotional when I read the passage with Jane and her young daughter.

I sincerely believe the loss of self is the essence of trauma. There seems to be many 'what ifs?' in people's lives, and I certainly know there are some in mine.

Chapter Eleven

Nigeria - part one

'When there is no enemy within, the enemy outside
cannot hurt you.'

- African Proverb -

August

The flight from Nairobi, Kenya, to Lagos, Nigeria, takes seven hours and fifteen minutes. I know nothing about Nigeria except what my husband told me. This was the primary country my husband was concerned about for my safety. He had two friends there who he trusted with his life. Henry, the Head of Security on the Palm Oil Plantation, and Paul, who was delegated to be with my husband throughout his stay in Nigeria as his personal bodyguard. Paul was part of Henry's security team. My husband had already arranged with them to protect me the whole time I would be staying in Nigeria. This part of my journey would no doubt be the most dangerous! I would live out on the Palm Oil Plantation for most of my stay, and partly in Owerri and Lagos. Nigeria is much bigger than I thought, with a population of two hundred and sixteen million.

Henry and Paul met me at Lagos airport. There was no question of misidentifying me with someone else at arrivals as I was the only westerner on the flight. The whole plane was taken up with Nigerians, not one other nationality. It isn't easy to enter Nigeria, unless you have a company to sponsor you because you are there on business, or you are being sponsored by somebody who resides there. We had to get a connecting flight from Lagos to Owerri in Imo State, a small town near the plantation, which takes one hour and ten minutes. It cost one hundred and ninety-four thousand naira for three people one way, which Henry paid. That's the equivalent of four hundred and fifty Canadian dollars. He told me that my husband had sent him money to cover any expenses for the duration of my stay, including his and Paul's salary, for my protection.

My husband was well received in Nigeria by the locals when he stayed here as he showed leadership skills and empathy; he wanted justice and fairness for everyone. He was Head of Security, but also had to stand in for the Managing Director, Neil, while he was away in Abuja and London on business meetings. Abuja is the capital of Nigeria, and suffers constant bombings in the city from the Boko Haram, a terrorist organisation based in north-eastern Nigeria. Neil is a buddy of my husband, who used to work with him while they were in the army together. Henry and Paul told me about some of the benevolent things my husband and Neil did for the community.

Paul told me a young Nigerian guy stole diesel from one of their jeeps to sell so he could go to his grandmother's funeral and bring some flowers. This guy was unemployed and did not have any money. My husband employed him as part of the security; he became one of his best security guys. When Neil and my husband took charge of managing the plantation and the operation of the mill, it was on its way to going bankrupt. But, they succeeded in getting the mill repaired and the workforce working efficiently, and started making a profit within six months. The boss who bought the plantation and the mill was Irish, giving them complete control of governing the entire enterprise. They were in their element, having the power to control things how they thought would be the most beneficial for all parties concerned.

Paul and Henry advised me that when I open a bottle

of some beverage and don't finish drinking it, if I should go away for a few minutes I should not come back and start drinking it again as some people could poison it. Also, when purchasing a bottle of drink, check the bottle's seal to ensure that it has not been tampered with because they could have put something in it. Also, the food cooked for me at the house by the maid or the tiny food stall outside the mill has to be checked for poison. I asked them why anyone would try and do this to me? To poison me or hurt me in any other way? They told me it was not just me but other people in their community. There were a few reasons, but they would tell me later. However, they also said that Nigerians wouldn't harm me if they didn't have a legitimate reason. They also assured me it is not like this everywhere in Nigeria, only in certain parts, just like in all countries worldwide. You have good areas and areas that you try and avoid. The same as corruption happening everywhere around the world, it also occurs here, and I have to be aware not to be scammed by anyone. My husband warned me about what happens here, but I didn't take it in when he told me. Paul reassured me everything would be fine, but I had to be vigilant, that's all.

Uneasiness started to creep up on me, and I started doubting myself again. Had I naively become too overconfident about what I could handle on my travels? I had a distinct feeling that this country would test me to my maximum. On the plantation, Henry allocated a small house with a maid to clean and cook for me. He had one of the security guards patrol around outside at night to ensure I was safe. A couple of days ago, Paul and Henry were walking with me through the Plantation, showing me the workers harvesting the bunches of Palm Oil fruit and loading the bunches on trucks. They told me that some guys climbing the trees to cut the bunches sometimes get bitten by poisonous snakes. If they get bitten on the neck, they have to get transported to the hospital as quick as possible. Promptness and speed are paramount; otherwise, they will die. They were not telling me this to scare me, they wanted me to be aware; even in the grass where we were walking there could be snakes. That same day, we witnessed some locals from the next village trying to steal some Palm Oil fruit bunches. We observed the plantation security having an altercation with them – both sides were ready to use their machetes. While witnessing this incident, I could feel my adrenalin start to flow. The only reason I didn't panic was that Paul and Henry were there.

It's mainly the unemployed and poor locals who steal the bunches, wanting to sell them on the black market. Palm oil is worth quite a bit of money. The bunches of fruit are about the size of an average man's torso and weigh approximately twenty-five to thirty kilograms. A ring road runs entirely around the boundary of the plantation, about sixty kilometres long, which the security vehicles patrol endlessly. The road is basically a dirt road, as are the rest of the roads winding throughout the plantation to the workers' tiny houses. Most workers ride bicycles to get to their respective places of work, like the mill, or the operation office to be allocated a particular part of the plantation to work that day. Some parents bring their children on small motorbikes to the school close to the mill. The other day, I observed a tumultuous crowd as I walked across the courtyard toward the school playground. As I got closer, I asked some women what the matter was. They said a young man was caught trying to sexually abuse a young woman behind the administrative offices.

Two men had hold of him, and one man behind hit the

culprit with a black rubber hose as they took him to the security office. The atmosphere was quite emotionally charged, with many women shouting abuse at him and the men being very aggressive. I had the urge to say something because it was escalating by the minute and getting entirely out of hand, but I didn't. The young guy was held at the security office until the police arrived. However, by the time the police arrived, he had been beaten by the young woman's father. Of course, sexual abuse happens in many countries, not just here.

Since living on the plantation, I've made some friends, and the people are always friendly and willing to help me. However, sometimes I feel isolated and lonely, miles away from the nearest town. But I chose to stay here purposely because I wanted to be in nature and away from the cities, so I had time to introspect. Every day I ate rice. My favourite was spicy jollof rice. With the rice I sometimes ate cassava, beans, or suya, which is a spicy grilled kebab, or puff-puff, which are fried sweet dough balls. Sometimes I had Ogbono soup, which is made from mango seeds. Every Sunday, most of the community on the plantation goes to church. After the service, Paul and I hand out candy to all the children. Candy is called *sweets here. Then, we drive out into the plantation to hand some out to the children who couldn't make it to church. It's become a regular thing for Paul and I to do this each Sunday. The children love it! After that, I get Paul or Henry to drive me into the town of Owerri, so I can go onto a computer to check my e-mails from my husband and daughter. Also to check my messages, as out on the plantation there is no connection to the Internet. Last Sunday, both Paul and Henry escorted me to the Marriott Hotel in Owerri, where it was possible to get a connection on the Internet to contact my husband and daughter. The hotel staff were always very friendly and asked how my family was doing, which I thought was nice. After sending messages to them, Paul, Henry and I had a beer and something to eat there. While eating, Henry and Paul mentioned they were concerned about me as I wasn't quite my usual self. I told them I felt a bit isolated and lonely out at the plantation, even though the locals always made me feel welcome. I thought going to the plantation and having some quiet time to reflect on my life would be ideal, but it didn't seem to be the case. They told me they would organise something with a guy called DJ to take me to Lagos for a few days and stay* with him and his wife to have a break from here. Currently, he is managing a team to install three boreholes in the plantation so the workers don't have to travel to the mill to collect water daily. He works for a few months here, then returns to Lagos for a few weeks, where his wife still lives and has a small food stall. He commutes between here and there regularly. I agreed with the idea and told them I would look forward to it. After finishing our meal, I opened the next brown envelope I had with me. I'd brought it especially to read out to them. I was hoping they would agree to give their opinions on the questions. They said yes without hesitation. So, I read the seven questions:

If you could turn back time, what choices would you make differently? What do you consider the biggest mistake of your life? What advice would you give your eight year old self? If you could change your career tomorrow, what would you choose? What is the one thing that drives you? What childhood trauma affects all your choices today? If you could only impart one lesson to your children, what would it be?

They both replied to some of the questions rather quickly. Then they thought about it for a while and started changing their responses. After a couple of minutes, they both decided if they could think about the questions more, they'd give me an answer later. So, I gave them the list of questions and felt flattered that they were taking them so earnestly. I noticed they were thought-provoking to them. But not just to them, they were to me, also.

Today I met with DJ, and Henry drove us to Owerri airport to catch the short flight to Lagos. Just behind the small airport car park is a row of about eight tiny kiosks, which accommodate approximately ten people, where you can sit down and have a snack and drink. Today is Friday, and we should return on Monday. DJ assured me he would protect me during our stay in Lagos. Henry knew I would be in good hands with him as he knew DJ had lived in Lagos for a good few years, and he knew his way around the area and what to look out for regarding dubious people. We had an hour before we checked in for our flight, so we sat in one of the kiosks and had a snack and a coffee. DJ told me that some people here love things and objects and use people, instead of loving people and using things and objects. Intimacy is on a downward trend due to corruption. You can't show *vulnerability, otherwise you will be used, ridiculed, or scammed. He told me to be constantly aware of my surroundings. I had noticed that DJ, Paul, and Henry were always observant. However, what DJ told me is also happening in society in many western countries nowadays.*

After our short one hour and fifteen minute flight, we landed at Lagos airport. When we left the airport, DJ flagged down two motorbike taxis to take us to his place. I had never been on a motorbike taxi before, so that was a unique experience. We arrived at the street where he lived with his wife. It was right out on the outskirts of Lagos in a rural area. The people lived in a row of wooden shacks on each side of the dirt road. We went into his place, dropped our small backpacks in his living room, and then made our way down the street to where his wife had her food stall. Although everyone we saw enroute seemed happy. We were surrounded by poverty. The houses in Owerri and on the plantation were made of bricks, but these were wooden shacks. I have to say, I was surprised. I was astonished at how they had to live here compared to where we had just come from.

DJ's wife was happy to see him again. As soon as I

saw them hugging, I immediately had thoughts of me arriving back in Canada and hugging my husband. She closed up her stall, and we all returned to their place to have something to eat. What she made was delicious. She spotted that I was taken aback by the situation in Lagos. She mentioned to DJ that he should take me to Abuja the next day, that I would enjoy that more. I felt embarrassed, but she made me feel at ease about the whole thing. She was a very kind and easy-going person, and I got along with her just fine.

The next day, DJ and I got a flight to Abuja, the capital of Nigeria, which took one hour and twenty minutes. Abuja was entirely different from Lagos. We stayed in a hotel near the airport and got a taxi into the city centre. Walking along the street, we were looking for a café to go into for coffee when we heard this massive explosion and saw the glass windows of the stores fly out onto the sidewalk and street about one hundred metres in front of us! Then, I could hear people screaming, alarm bells going off from various stores, and police sirens; it was mayhem! We quickly hailed a taxi and went straight back to the hotel. We watched the news on the TV in the hotel lobby to see what was happening. They stated that the bomb was initiated by the terrorist organisation Boko Haram.

The next day, DJ and I got the first available flight back to Owerri. What a weekend! When we landed, DJ phoned Henry to come and collect us from the airport. However, Henry was at the police station in Owerri and told us to stay overnight at the hotel as he was busy with a significant incident with Paul, the security team, and the police.

Apparently, two men heard that a particular policeman in Owerri had inherited a substantial amount of money. They kidnapped him, took him out into the middle of the plantation, and demanded a ransom from his family. However, the family told the kidnappers that the information about him receiving a considerable amount of money was fake news and that they would be unable to pay the ransom they demanded. The security team and police had been searching the plantation to try and find the kidnappers and the kidnapped policeman for the last seventy-two hours with no positive result. Of course, the area is massive; it was no wonder it was taking so long.

Paul came to the hotel the next day to pick us up and

take us back to the plantation. We arrived at the security office first to check in with Henry. We all sat down and had a coffee while Henry explained in more detail what had happened since I had left to go to Lagos. No sooner than he started to explain, the security van drove up with a couple of the security guys and the kidnapped policeman. As soon as the kidnappers had found out that they couldn't get any money from the family in return for him, they left him tied up in the middle of the plantation. When the security guys found him, he was completely dehydrated. I told them he had to go straight to the hospital as quickly as possible, because he was deficient in crucial electrolytes. Another critical factor is that when you are dehydrated, your blood thickens, and there is a possibility of a stroke or heart attack.

I like Jane's decisiveness and ability to make decisions quickly and effectively. She has the discipline to remain focused and steadfast to achieve a result. That's her nursing experience emerging. The situation is different here, compared to the incident in China on the train platform. In this incident, she is somewhat in control as she is relying on her nursing experience and not feeling helpless.

The next day, the Headmaster of the school on the plantation asked me if I would mind standing in for the school nurse for a few days as she had to attend her mother's funeral in her home village about forty kilometres away. She had died of a severe case of malaria. I agreed; I just needed a day to rest up and recover from the incidents I had encountered over the last couple of days.

Today, I was in the school nurse's office, sifting through some medicines kept in the medicine cabinet. I looked out the open window and watched the kids playing on the playground – a grassed area with an old tree lying where some kids can sit. They all looked to be happy and enjoying themselves, even though they haven't got much, just an old vehicle tyre, a football, and some sticks to play with. As I looked at the kids playing, I began to quietly laugh to myself. Almost a year ago, I was in a big hospital in Canada as a nurse, and here I am in the middle of a Palm Oil Plantation in Nigeria as a replacement school nurse; how surreal. It was a defining moment for me that I, or anybody who really wanted to, could go anywhere and do anything, within reason. It was a liberating feeling that this was possible. It showed *me that many of us believe we are incapable of doing many things, but fear, in the end, holds us back – not that we are incompetent. The incidents of the last few days had changed me; I was seeing the world from a different perspective, as though somebody had grabbed me and shaken a tiny bit of naivety out of me, and I was grateful for that.*

Chapter Twelve

Nigeria - part two

'The most difficult thing in life is to know yourself.'

- Thales -

September - October

Today I've decided to sit in front of the house underneath one of the coconut trees with its vast leaves above, draping over me as its shade protects me from the sun. I'm taking some time out to read a little from one of my books and write a few pages in my journal. But the first thing I'm going to do is open the next brown envelope and read the seven questions:

Which country would you move to if you had the resources right now? Where do you see yourself happiest? Do you do things with intention, or are you simply going through the motions of mundane life? Would your thirteen year old self be proud of you right now? Is there something you've always wanted to learn, and what's stopping you? What question would you like to ask someone to which you are afraid of the answer?

What parts of your life are you deeply unsatisfied with?

I'm nearing the end of my journey. This is the last big push, and before I return home, I have to figure out how my life will continue back in Canada. I realise I'm the creator of my life, but what would I do if I could live anywhere in the world? What job? I need autonomy to express myself and be creative. A counsellor, perhaps?

I love reading books and writing. I would like to become a freelance writer.

I sat there to quietly introspect for a while. I let my higher self talk to me. After having so many conversations with all the people I've met on my travels, I've discovered that everybody's life is a story. A story is not simply what happens; it includes the meaning of what happens. Don't let others define you. The world will ask you who you are; if you don't know, the world will tell you. Find your true beliefs and values. Ask who you really are. Are you more introverted or extroverted? What are your strengths and weaknesses? What are your values and beliefs? Be truthful about all aspects of yourself to find out who you really are. Find your voice, nobody else's.

Show the world who you really are. Understand your

passions. Focus on who you want to be. Choose who you want to become and strive in life to be that person. Give up your addictions. Every form of addiction is wrong. Be honest about your capabilities. You are what you do, not what you say you'll do. We are rarely who we pretend we will be. What we do speaks for ourselves much louder than anything we communicate verbally. Who do I really want to be? Make strengths from your weaknesses. Find connection to the infinite. Make time for deep reflections. Solitude is one of the best ways to heal oneself. It would be best if you were alone to find out what supports you when you find that you cannot support yourself. What truly makes you happy, satisfied, and content?

Concentrate on that. What matters to you? Connect with what matters to you. The journey through your entire life has constantly been struggling with your dark side, your shadow side. But you must eventually accept it. Ninety-five percent of what you do is driven by your subconscious. However, it would help if you unlearned old beliefs and values that do not serve you anymore and learn new ones. Finding meaning is essential in your job. Your life is simply not just what happens; it includes the meaning of what happens. We are all wearing masks. The persona we display to the outside world is partly false because society expects that from us – and because we feel too vulnerable to show what we think is our true self to the outside world. And why? It's mostly down to fear. Fear of being ridiculed, or the fear of someone breaking off being your friend. Or, being afraid somebody will use and manipulate you for their own good. It all comes back to fear. Most people don't even know they are living a false persona they think is theirs, but, deep down, they are not happy with this persona because they suspect this is not really them, and at some point in their life they detect this, which usually starts them on a quest to find out who they genuinely are. At first, this can be problematic because all the family and friends start noticing a different you, not the you they are familiar with. This can cause conflict. The past drives us to say and do certain things in life. Ninety-five percent of our unconscious drives our emotions, feelings, and actions in life, both positive and negative.

Wow, Jane's epic journey of eleven months of experiences and the wisdom she's learned along the way has definitely paid off. I've got to read that again. Jane, you do not realise how much you have helped me, maybe even healed me to some extent. Jane has, without a doubt, what people call resilience. She can rapidly return to her emotional and mental state baseline after stressful, traumatic, or triumphant events.

I haven't mentioned anything to my husband or daughter about any of the incidents that have been happening to me since I've been in Nigeria because they would worry themselves sick. I told Henry and Paul not to say anything, either.

Over the next few days, I walked with Paul on the dirt tracks through the plantation for hours on end. It's quiet and peaceful, and we chat about this and that.

After reading what Jane endured whilst being in Nigeria, I've tried to introspect between reading parts of Jane's journal, but I have trepidation in finding out something I don't want to deal with. I'm afraid to be entirely honest with myself because I'm anxious about what I might discover. I'm nervous about allowing my dark and shadow sides to surface, even though I think it is integral to me. I conceal it in a painful attempt to protect the narrative that I decide to show the outside world. Fear of the unknown always holds me back. I have to find, understand, and accept my shadow side so I can control it and not let it control me.

When I first arrived at the plantation, Henry and Paul told me to get a small bag and pack it with essential items like my passport, money, and any other valuables, and for me to hide it. Only Henry, Paul, and myself knew where it was. This would be called my 'go bag'. If an emergency situation occurred, I was to immediately collect my 'go bag' and make my way to a predestined location where we would rendezvous, which they named the RV. They would meet me there and drive me as quickly as possible to Owerri airport. This sounded very clandestine to me, but they assured me this was the most effective procedure when there would be an imminent threat to my life. They told me my husband had undergone the same process with them.

As Paul and I were strolling through the plantation, I felt a sharp pain in my leg. Paul said he was sure I'd been bitten by a poisonous snake. He ran off as fast as he could to get the security vehicle. He drove me to the nearest hospital, located just outside Owerri. Time was of the essence. I was starting to feel dizzy and thought I would pass out. Antivenom is the treatment for severe snake envenomation. The sooner antivenom can be started, the sooner irreversible damage from venom can be stopped. The hospital is adequately equipped to deal with this situation, as snake bites are an almost daily occurrence.

As we approached Owerri, construction work was being carried out on the road due to the amount of rain they'd received over the monsoon season, which was approximately three months of almost continuous rain. We had to take a detour, which costed us precious time. I was passing in and out of consciousness. Faced with death, you quickly discover your truth. What has the most meaning for you, what do you value most, and what do you wish you had and hadn't done in your life? Your values get prioritised very quickly, coming to terms with a very short future when you know you will die soon.

As soon as we arrived at the hospital, I got rushed into the emergency room. Beside me was a woman with severe malaria and typhoid; she was very weak and sweating profusely. It looked like she could die any minute. She turned her head and smiled at me as we lay there next to each other. I was sure I recognised her; she was one of the workers who used to pick her daughter up from the school on the plantation. I was passing in and out of consciousness more frequently by this time. The woman told me about her regrets and what she wished she had done in her life. She asked what I would do if I had only months left to live. So many thoughts raced through my head to give her and me an honest answer. I thought of all the things I'd like to do or see and specific friends I'd like to see before it was too late. Then, I answered her I would spend that precious time with the people who were always there for me when I needed someone, and who unquestionably loved me for who I was, flaws and all. That would be two people and those people I have unconditional love for: my husband and daughter. The woman smiled. I was then compelled to tell this woman what I had told my sister-in-law in the UK. I don't know why I felt I had to do this, but I did. Many years ago, when my husband and I had just recently gotten married, I had a miscarriage. I felt melancholic when this happened, thinking, why did this happen to us? We were good people; we never did any harm to anyone. The dying woman told me it wasn't the right time for my daughter to be born. But the right time was when she was eventually born into the world. Everything happens in the right place at the right time for a reason.

We both looked into each other's eyes longer than one usually would, which would have made the other person uncomfortable, but this moment wasn't awkward; it was wisdom shining through this dying woman's eyes. A hard-working woman with dignity who had experienced much hardship in her life to survive. She had been a strong and loving mother whose time was coming to an end. The Nigerian woman asked me if I would read out a specific eulogy at her funeral. She was clasping a small bible in her left hand; she opened it up, pulled a folded piece of paper out, and handed it to me. It looked as though she had kept this piece of paper for a long time because where it had been folded was very worn and starting to fall apart. This is what was written on the piece of paper:

'No one wants to die. Even people who want to go to heaven don't want to die to get there. And yet, death is the destination we all share. No one has ever escaped it, and that is how it should be, because death is very likely the single best invention of life. It's life's change agent. It clears out the old to make way for the new.'

I recognised this statement; it was from Steve Jobs.

I glanced over at her and wanted to say something, but nothing came out. Then it went dark, very quickly.

Then completely black.

My name is Henry, and when Miss Jane arrived at the plantation, she instructed me that if anything were to happen to her, I would fetch her journal and bring it to her so she could write something to her husband, Mr. James, and their daughter. If she couldn't write something due to some tragic incident, I was to ensure the journal got back to her husband, Mr. James, safely, and then inform him that Miss Jane had left a personal letter for him and their daughter in her bedside cabinet drawer at their home. As soon as I heard from Paul what had happened, I rushed to get the journal, and Paul picked me up at the plantation's main entrance gates, and then carried on to the hospital. I started writing in Miss Jane's journal the minute I got in the security vehicle; she dictated, and I wrote everything for her. I wrote for her right up until she died.

She was dead for approximately fourteen minutes before the doctors revived her. She told us that she had an NDE. Near Death Experience. I had never heard of this before. She told us she had met the lady next to her in a tranquil place and that they talked about personal things. The woman did, in actual fact, die shortly after

Miss Jane. Did they meet up again after death, or is there another explanation for Miss Jane's mystical experience?

Paul and I have been at the hospital for two days; we take turns being by her side. She is still dictating to me what to write as she has still not fully recovered. Tomorrow she will be discharged from the hospital, but the doctor told her she still has to rest and drink plenty of fluids.

Chapter Thirteen

Canada - back in time for Thanksgiving

'A man travels the world over in search of what he needs and returns home to find it.'

- George A. Moore -

October

Henry and Paul are organising a farewell for my last night in Nigeria. They have invited all the workers and the administrative staff from the plantation. There'll be approximately three hundred people. Henry asked me if, on the night, I could give a small speech and share some of the wisdom that I had learnt on my travels over the last twelve months. I had two days to prepare what I would say that evening.

The evening of the party had tables full of food and drink. There was a small area cornered off where people could dance to Nigerian music. After about an hour, they stopped the music, and someone from the administration got up and said a few words about me, then a few words about my husband, whom they all knew from his time here years ago. They then handed me the microphone to share some of the wisdom I had learnt on my travels over the last twelve months. After thanking them for their hospitality whilst residing at the plantation, I proceeded with my two minute talk. However, I didn't mention any of the countries I had been to. Instead, I told them how fortunate I was to be able to spend time in their community. I'd learnt a lot about myself by spending time in Nigeria. As I was just about to finish, I said, "I will end this talk with the last seven questions from my friend. My dear friend, whom I learned yesterday died of cancer."

They were: what social issue resonates most with you? If you could never fail, what are the things you would absolutely do? Where does the concept of justice come from? Is it man-made or natural for every living being? What can we teach our students so our future will have more peace? How many real friends do you have, and who can you genuinely count on when you desperately need help? Do you consider me a friend?

Underneath the questions, she'd written her last quote for me:

'Time is the coin of life, spend it well.' Carl Sandburg.

Over twelve months of reading all her questions, I never got around to answering them except the last one. Yes, you are my best friend! Rest In Peace.

Arriving back in Canada after experiencing so many countries and various cultures seemed alien to me, almost as though it was a different place. A memory so faint I could barely remember it. The scenery looked foreign to me after seeing so many other landscapes over the past year. I noticed a significant transformation in myself; I perceived everything differently. I wasn't the same person as when I'd left a year ago. I had to get an earlier flight than the one I told my husband and daughter I would be on. As much as I miss them, I haven't told them yet. I want to go to the cabin and spend some time alone before I call them to meet me there. Tomorrow is Thanksgiving. Fitting. The cabin was where my epic journey started and where it will shortly end.

I think of what people worry about in Canada, and their concerns about petty things compared to what is happening in Nigeria and other parts of the world. In most first-world countries, some people are concerned that there isn't enough milk in their caffe latte, or that they must wait a short while in line before getting served, or that there is a tiny hairline scratch on their car. People in these countries don't know how good they have it. I arranged with Mr. Smith last year that I would rent the cabin for this Thanksgiving and asked if he could get some supplies for me and drop them off there.

I'm at the cabin now and have just made a cup of coffee. I am looking at photos on my phone from the last twelve months of travelling. What a year! This will probably be the last entry in my journal. I am so looking forward to seeing my family tomorrow! I've missed them!

Jane has travelled worldwide and returned with physical, mental, and spiritual knowledge to evolve and move forward with her life. Unknowingly, she has dragged me along with her. She has transformed my mindset, and I feel I am shedding my childhood and moving into adulthood. We have both experienced the death of the old self and reunited with our genuine true selves, which we disengaged from long ago. Jane slayed the dragon, so she could go into the cave and obtain the treasure. One of the valuable lessons I learnt from Jane is that it is helpful if you can be centred and not act out of desire or fear.

We spend time compulsively seeking something that

will give our lives meaning and purpose, for example: religion, romance, and work. Because, in this life drama, people's lives make no sense to them; they must justify their existence. You know you're on the right path when you are in a position where you don't betray yourself.

I will try and find Jane and return her journal to her, and because Jane likes her quotes, I have found something on the internet from Rumi, who I know she likes. I will write this on a piece of paper and put it between the last pages of her journal.

'1. What is Poison? Anything which is more than our necessity is poison. It may be power, wealth, hunger, ego, greed, laziness, love, ambition, hate or anything.

'2. What is Fear? Non-acceptance of uncertainty. If we accept that uncertainty, it becomes Adventure.

'3. What is Envy? Non-acceptance of good in others, if we accept that good, it becomes Inspiration.

'4. What is Anger? Non-acceptance of things which are beyond our control. If we accept, it becomes Tolerance.

'5. What is Hatred? Non-acceptance of a person how they are. If we accept a person unconditionally, it becomes Love.

'6. Nothing is greater than the story, and nobody is greater than the story. The story is the sun, and the characters are flowers, and the story allows the characters to blossom.'

It has been two years since I returned to Canada after my journey of a lifetime. And I have just met Sarah; she has returned my journal, which I misplaced two years ago at the cabin. Not in a million years did I think I would be making another entry into my journal, but here I am again. Sarah managed to find and make contact with my daughter, which led her to me. I am so happy to have my journal back. Sarah is studying journalism at university and has asked me if she can get my permission to write a book about my story and the journal. I'm writing the epilogue entry into my journal today, so she can start writing the first draft of the manuscript next week. Since I've been back, my daughter has gotten married and given birth to a lovely baby girl. They live here in Ontario, now. I work part-time as a counsellor for young adults, and my daughter helps out part-time at the café. When my daughter works at the café, I care for her baby. Between all that, I do a little bit of gardening. For one whole year, I searched for my authentic self, what vocation I should do and where. I've found all that now and am totally satisfied and content. I believe in Sarah, too. She was in a dark place two years ago, but she's found her passion in writing. She's still working on who she exactly is, but she'll get there. We've all decided to spend Thanksgiving together at the cabin this year, including Sarah. She has given me a women's magazine, which has a section for potential professional writers to write an article on something they believe is worth expressing. I want to insert Sarah's article as the final entry into my journal:

It's All About Stories

Everything has a story. Because we live inside a story. Our lives are made up of stories. We need meaning to make sense of the story, and meaning is more important than anything else. Some stories are about freedom and change. People feel satisfied in their comfort zone, afraid of losing their old story. Most people feel trapped in their stories in one way or another. But they are not. If they want to be free, to have freedom, they have to take responsibility. In most people's stories, they say they want to change. But what they really want is for the other characters in their story to change. The majority of people don't want to change because of the loss of the familiar, the loss of their old story that identifies them, even if it is totally unpleasant. You have to edit your old story by unlearning the narrative you have been telling yourself before going on to the next chapter of your life. Some of us travel to search for something; we're not sure what, but for one woman I know, it was seeking her authentic self, and for her purpose and meaning at this stage of her life. Our future is up to us. Shed the old story of you to experience something more unique and better. Her travelling to various countries for a year was like healing an open wound. I have noticed that everyone sees the same things but perceives them differently. Purpose and meaning in life are personal things. The purpose is so profoundly personal because it is related to yourself as a human being and your experiences through life.

Everybody needs meaning in their life, otherwise, you question: what's the point? You have to realise the tiny spark you have inside you. Then you can do something about it. Some people live under mass hypnosis. In society, you're kept in your place as a consumer to be happy. You're in a kind of trance. A number of us, when we come home from working the whole day, usually sit down and watch TV until it's time to go to bed. However, we probably work at a job we hate, so we can buy items we don't need to impress people we don't like. All to please your ego? When participating in something you don't enjoy, you lose your creativity; you can't express the real you. You are told early on what to do and what not to do. Everything is dictated to you – a form of conditioning.

Society expects you to go to school, then college and university, and work for some big corporation at a job you more than likely don't enjoy and are not satisfied with to pay off your huge mortgage – instead of doing the work you enjoy and would be satisfied and content doing. There needs to be a death of the old you, like a snake shedding its skin so the new you can emerge. There has to be the death of your old narrative, so something living can carry on. Follow your bliss. What would you do if you had all the time and money? What stops you from following your bliss? Is it the fear of what people would say about you? Is it rejection or ridicule that you are afraid of? Even if you try to find what you are supposed to do in your life and don't succeed, isn't that a worthy cause in itself? The choice is yours – it's always yours! The fear is the demons and dragons inside you that must be slain. Courage is to move forward and explore the unknown. The protagonist is you, and your ego is the antagonist. When we overcome our fears, we gain power. The whole journey of life is about self-discovery. Souls tend to go back to those who feel like home. You need to be curious about everything. Ask questions, question everything. Philosophy is storytelling, so people can learn something. You can have a simple life, but you need purpose and meaning. You have to overcome your fears to transform into becoming your authentic self. Stand for something. You need to connect to a particular group of people. It would be helpful for you to see life in stages, such as the four seasons. We have to make sure we take the time to savour every season. Take time to savour the smell of coffee in the mornings when you get up. Enjoy the experiences you have every day as much as possible. Follow your dreams, passions, and talents so you won't have any regrets. Loving and accepting yourself as you are is a decisive moment because that lines you up directly with the universe, and then there is no more war inside you. As that gap heals between the unlovable self, you gain power in life. Joseph Campbell once said, 'The privilege of a lifetime is being who you are.'

In an adventure, a journey, there's a circle which has to be completed. You have to return to where you started. To return with the treasure, – the treasure being: tell your story – we need to wake up to our potential. Some of us are in a slumber. We don't realise the potential we have. Expectations can be problematic because you are disappointed when they are not met. Also, wanting instant gratification all the time can lead to addiction. Loners are self-aware due to all the time spent alone looking within and introspecting. So, while others ignore or run away from their emotions, loners choose to focus on them. This is what helps them get to know themselves better than most people.

People who prefer to be alone have incredible strength and willpower, almost envied by others. They know how to handle challenging situations because of their time in self-reflection. We need a group of people, a family or the equivalent, where we feel safe and know someone will help us when we need it. People need an inhabitant where they feel they belong. Everyone has a story to tell;

you must take the time to listen. Perhaps we can learn something from it. At a certain age, when you experience situations, places, and people, you realise deep inside you, with that instinctive gut-knowing feeling, that it will be the last time that you see that special friend or a family member. There will be a mixture of emotions: sadness knowing you will never see them again, and joyfulness that you had the privilege of spending time with them and enjoying their company. Some people say everything is energy. We don't die; we go back to the (our) source. It's lovely when kids leave home and go their own way – we've all gone one step further forward in the game of life. Parents realise their children are getting more robust, confident, and intelligent, and they, the parents, are slowly deteriorating in body and mind. This is the cycle of life.

Parents notice their children have overtaken them. Their children are on the way up, and they are on the way down; they meet briefly in the middle, and then they drift slowly apart. Some of us have observed over the years that people want to escape what they believe is their humdrum life for a more exciting one. They're just going from whistling one tune to whistling another. Most people think and feel they don't impact anyone, but they do. Anger is a repressed feeling; it's not really about what's happening now. It originates primarily from your childhood's unresolved issues. Your emotions don't care about the facts, and the facts don't care about your feelings. The highest vibration to achieve is knowing you have peace, not necessarily money or possessions. Perseverance is the constancy of doing something despite difficulty or delay in achieving success. Humans can die way before their heart stops beating. We die when we stop feeling useful. To discover who we are, we must peel back the layers of identities we have taken on over the years. However, people are reluctant to do this out of fear; they are concerned they will excavate something they don't want to see or feel, and then have to deal with it. They try and avoid this confrontation. It's fear of the unknown. But to discover our true identity, we must dig and dig deep.

We need to silence the voices in our heads. They are not us. They are what we have heard from the government, teachers, parents, etc. You must find your voice and nobody else's and listen to it. To do this, listen in silence. If I listen to my voice, my essence, nobody can affect me. When you have found your voice, you have found your authentic self! You will then know what to do with your life.

Enjoy the process of your journey more than the destination. Ask, doubt everything. Self-love is essential; not being able to do this must be agony. Life is a process constantly changing. Don't look for the right door; look for the right key. The key is you! Focus on the key! Otherwise, it's all a waste of time.

'We are like books. Most people only see our cover, the minority read only the introduction, many believe the critics. Few will know our content.' Emile Zola.

Before I hand over my journal to Sarah for her to make a start on the manuscript, we would both like to insert one last quote each.

'A book is a magical thing that lets you travel to far-away places without ever leaving your chair.' Theodor Seuss Geisel.

'Writing is the geometry of the soul.' Plato.

I'll let you figure out who inserted which quote…

Love, Jane x

About the Author

Paul Newman was born in Ipswich in the United Kingdom in 1959. He has a keen interest in psychology, sociology, and philosophy. He served in the Royal Engineers of the British Army. Subsequently, he is employed as a worldwide Security Manager and Consultant. Over the last forty years, he has visited forty-four countries, some in remote, dangerous places, primarily due to his work. In 2023 he will be going into semi-retirement, so he will be able to write more books!

Paul's favourite activities are running, cross-country skiing, reading, and writing. His special interests and skills lie in motivating people and explaining specific subject matter. He has a passion for learning and anything to do with adventure.

Written in Ink is Paul's first fiction book.

www.blossomspringpublishing.com